Nomads of the Alley

a novella

two short stories
The Sad Life of John Adams
The Trees

Michael Conway

Published by Former Quarter Ton Man

www.formerquartertonman.com

Conway, Michael
Nomads of the Alley a novella & two short stories, Michael Conway

ISBN 978-0-578-03218-4 (pbk.)

This book is dedicated to my wife who remains beautiful and listens to my rants.

Nomads of the Alley

a novella

Night of the Rat

Rat burrowed daylight hours away with his community beneath one of the many bridges dissecting the Pike. Speeding vehicles made the cement shoulder shimmer but Rat and the rats did not mind for it rocked them to sleep. They slept while Two Leggers shuttled to and from their tedious places of dread. The clan ate well at night, the hours when rats bid for food and fun. One frigid night, leaving rats scurrying for food and warmth, Rat witnessed a crime. Here is the crime he happened upon during the winter of '99.

With limited knowledge of the city's signs, names or logos, Rat was fortunate being instinctively privy to the abundances of discarded food. Chinatown, scuttling toward Harrison Avenue on short hairy legs, peripatetic as rats chose to be, he made use of the gutter so not to be noticed by the Two Leggers. He skipped down the dozen stairs at the walkway's end between the hospital and Wang Center. Aromatic garbage exhalations journeyed to the nose of the rat. He followed Pork Lo Mein and the like cooked the previous night by Mr. Po. He arrived at the dumpster to find dozens of rats ripping at the veggies, noodles and meat. Not wanting a jam with the Tyler Street Rats, he quietly guffawed and proceeded on his way.

Long whiskers, gray like the eyes of Betty the Whore, sledded up Boylston for another dumpster a few blocks over. Rat became euphoric when he arrived at the alley lacking a rodent soup line. He leapt skyward landing sharp claws on the edge of the rusted cubicle. He free fell into the slime and soon his stomach extended. Like a Two Legger he belched then lay lethargic.

Rat continued to binge when a noise made him instinctively freeze. Rodent adrenaline traveled within his oiled skin to discern fight or flight. He leapt back to the edge and watched Two Leggers scuffle. Eventually one ran out of the alley while the other slid down the brick wall grabbing his gut, next to a door leading to nowhere. The man on the ground glared at the rat. Horrified, Rat ran back to his home beneath the bridge, never to report the crime, nor would he if within his vocabulary.

Leonard Turkleton, 1988

At twenty-three years of obesity, Leonard Turkleton sauntered into the Stage School, plopped down and sat for an interview with a man adorning oversized ears. The man once had delusions of stardom but theatrical crowds would not have it. Rejected, he started his own acting school, became a conman and drunk. Leonard studied the man's demeanor, dress, and surroundings. A true artist, he surmised.

"Leonard, I think you have talent. With precise training, direction, and a little push, you could work in commercials," the man informed in Southern drawl.

Yet, the conman had never been further than Hoboken when directing a high school play. Pondering the high-spirited pitch, Leonard peered beyond the receded hairline, to across the street where homeless men prepared for battle. Three had surrounded one and Leonard imagined the one had taken too long a swig from the army green bottle. They moved like Keystone Cops on valium, varying in intervals of time.

"So what do you think Mister Turkleton?" asked the crustacean who sensed losing his crowd.

Unbelieving of the man's positive predictions, Leonard quietly sighed. He impulsively stuffed money into the bottom feeder's claw, and exited the room for the quagmire across the street. Black and white headshots as witness, the conman pawed the money and grinned. For it would buy dinner at the diner, a whore at the whorehouse. Dinner would be bought last.

Leonard descended the Vaudevillian papered stairwell, smashed through the door, and crossed the street to watch the men slug it out. Arriving at the alley, Leonard was baffled. The group was now hugging and cheery, reinstating pledges of those in the alleys, gutters and streets. He could not understand these men in tattered fatigues, and departed.

Clouds marched north over Quincy and Neponset, soon to blanket the Zone. The sky was haziest nearest the sun. Leonard ambled toward the subway where odors reminded him of hookers and whores working high above the tracks. His fat face marquee the disgust of humidity. He stopped upon noticing another alley that appeared a black crack between buildings of finance. At the noon time hour, it reminded him of the skin encapsulating Betty the Whore, or so he remembered of her. He decided to enter her womb.

His eyes adjusted and coolness surrounded him. He studied the scene. An old Coke can, now yellow, lay atop a pyramid of garbage in the corner. Newer brick encased a onetime loading dock. A working, cast iron fire escape, hung from the left wall. Stains of grime beneath his sneakers. An octagonal sign warned what would happen if you parked here.

Imagination clipped his mind.

This he imagined. The can had arrived at this place after decades of being kicked by humans, students, and mice. Its dent? Achieved when a monstrous rat played kick the can. Rouge wooden chips lay scattered in the dark, remnants of a onetime loading dock hermetically sealed by the Cataldo Construction Co. during the Great Depression. Stains on the ground, blood of a whore. The fire escape journeyed to and from nowhere like the lives of men and rats. The octagonal sign, apocalyptic warning to patrons of the Zone. Leonard looked high above to notice a small window. He decided to move before the supposed banker jumped. A noise chinked somewhere in the alley. Leonard expedited a departure. Darkness followed him out of the alley. Depression inched its way in.

In the streets of reality, Leonard weaved through a parade of cars then stood at the intersection lights where heat fried overused engines. Testosterone driven punks heckled Betty the Whore, dressed in green like a sex superhero. In the confines of an old Caddy a pimp slapped his bitch for coming up short. He slapped her again. The slaps turned to fists closing her left eye shut. The whore sat there helpless like decades prior when Uncle manipulated her pajamas and mind. Betty watched from the corner, turned and walked the other way, inviting overused engines from their cars.

Aside the *DO NOT WALK* at Washington and Essex, a john inquired of Tina the Whore, "What will ten get me this after'?"

Warrior paint eyes squinted, pillow lips became thin and stretched, "Crumble it up and stick it up your fuckin' ass pervert," she returned.

Her pimp, J, remained calm and ready up the block.

The pavement showboating all of this began to rumble. Leonard attempted to run but obesity slowed him. Then two flights down and a

7

turnstile to be fed, Leonard thirsted for escape from this place, not the Zone itself, but daylight hours, his least favorite time to be there.

He winced sourly having missed the train. A beer gut will do that every time, he thought. Forced to smell the platform reeking of Tina's urine fermented cunt, Leonard recalled the wine weak men who titillated him earlier. His head filled with doom thinking them poster children, misfits of the lost. Vomit covered stubble, leathery cheeks, a snapshot of hell. He imagined them nomads.

Leonard believed himself different from most that passed this land way short of paradise. As most regarded people of the alleys as losers or byproducts of quirky genes, Leonard believed them to be nomads on some type of journey. Yet, the place to where they traveled was beyond his fantasies.

He sat on a corroded wooden bench, *Chico & Georgia 86*, despair filling him like a rat's belly at a Chinese buffet. To deal with the onslaught of unwanted feelings, historically prone to do, Leonard daydreamed of food. He recalled the Vietnamese joint up the block, spicy rice, meat skewered on splintered sticks. An orange train screeched to a halt. Leonard sat inside the filthy vehicle and twisted his month old beard. Fear misted through him as he thought of the men grappling in the alley. I wonder how they got there. He daydreamed of food to escape the unease, the train and his mind, a parallel exodus.

Ingesting three sandwiches, strawberry ice cream, and two liters of soda, Leonard napped in his home until the brightness of day faded to mauve, then periwinkle. Purple, he rose to capture his weekly fix of porn.

He backtracked the same transits and waits to the station reeking of Tina. He climbed two flights and huffed into the street. Euphoria invaded synapses as Leonard scanned the immediate section of Combat Zone, her neon lights whispering lies like the dining and whoring conman. Come to me, she said.

Leonard quietly announced to no one, "I love this place."

First things first he decided. He sat in the Vietnamese joint chopsticking sodium blow into his oversized ankles. Leaving change for the six-dollar meal, the proprietor's daughter gave Turk a wink. He wiped his face with a red napkin, tossed it into the grimy red bucket, and exited for the red blinking streets. Dessert would follow at the 24-hour porn theater.

The entrance now mere yards away, his head buzzed with excitement as he approached the Pilgrim Theatre. *Now Showing* and *Coming Soon* posters beckoned behind windowed tombs to the right and left, their walls slowly angling for the door like a funnel. Immediately inside he handed the familiar old man five dollars through the half-moon opening in the plexiglass. Obese Leonard took his *Admit One*, slightly turned, and smashed his hip into the turnstile. The man looked up from his paper, nodded his head, and adjusted the radio to better hear the game.

A perpendicular sign warned Leonard what the Boston Police would do if he solicited sex or showed lude or lascivious conduct. A man stumbled by and approached the half-mooned glass.

"I want my money back," the patron demanded. "Those posters aren't the ones playing."

The employee counted one-dollar bills, scanned for a winning horse, never acknowledging the plaintiff.

"Fuck you," yelled the drunk, and stumbled out the door.

Leonard no longer heard the Celtics but the bass rattling moans enticing him to venture beyond the cinema door. He entered the darkness where giants fucked on the screen. Passing a chest high wall where men leaned their elbows, ballplayers waiting to be called into the game, Leonard sat two rows into the darkness. He retrieved a half pint of Absolute and took a long chug. His belly burned. A brief time later, his face numbed and grinned. Statistically not a fighter, when drinking Leonard thought himself Caligula.

Blackened figures sat in seats and stood against the walls. Tiny orange lights intermittently flickered from the tips of cigarettes, followed by hacks and spit. Old men grunted having just spent their seed into a younger mouth or condom. Bleach smelling puddles swam on the slow sloping floor. Fucking, and fucking echoes, echoed from the screen. Figures congregated near one of the many pillars aligning the aisles to watch one man giving many others head. They hoped the kneeling man could take another in his mouth, face or hair. Sleepers, nappers, sobering-ups announced states of somnolence with grunts, jerks and sighs. Occasional vomit. A large black man received head as he slept. Leonard watched it all. Men sat alone. Together. In groups. The tinkling sound of fallen nips, rolling until they end in a puddle. Near the fire door a man stroked himself. Others swarmed to him like a virus. All of this and more loomed behind the well-lit marquee of the Pilgrim. Leonard enjoying it all, until something ran over his foot and out he went.

"You got fuckin' rats in there," he told the half-moon.

"I know," said the man still picking horses.

"Well?" demanded Leonard. The man said nothing else.

Fucking rats. Fuckin' rats! What the fuck! Leonard screamed. Then he left.   He crossed the street and sat on a cold cement bench. Alcohol mingled with his mood making for the worse. Saturday night, middle of the Zone, Leonard thought of his departed mother.

She died when Leonard attended high school. The following months he imploded with fat. Isolation followed. Fat. Meaningless menial jobs. And hence, he was sitting on a bench in the Combat Zone having conversations with neon signs, thinking of Ma.

He wanted more alcohol, so walked across to the Naked I. Three Peppermint Schnapps, a vague chat with a waitress about nothing, he sat alone in a small booth. He watched the strippers come and go off the small stage wondering how they bent backward like that. He looked around at the dark place and thought once again of his mother. I miss you, he said to her deadness.   Numbness overcame him. Depression coupled with alcohol distorted his thoughts. He left the club, its darkness and one-dollar bills, and descended two flights into Tina's reek.

Leonard waited for the train, and waited. Standing at the platform's edge, cognitions readying to jump, he thought of sex, childhood, Father, Mother, strippers, God. Daydreaming of food, his mind blackened like an all night porn theater. He remembered nothing else.

Sunday passed Leonard swimming in vomit.

Monday arrived and Leonard slept until noon as if he had each working day. Moments before twelve, tick, tick, tick, ring. He awoke from his fitful apnea and reached for the old heavy phone. It was his alarm clock, Linda, his girlfriend of three months. Ring, ring...

Following Mother's death, and prior to meeting Linda, Turkleton prone to watching porn, equated giants fucking and sucking at the Pilgrim as love; a primal act portrayed by actors who later died of self inflicted gunshots, overdoses, or tentacles of hungry virus. He found this same love in dirty magazines. Realistic love, that which he had with mother, now seemed unattainable. It fleeted like the money he spent on the industry of sex. Then she simply arrived. He thought she would save him from the loneliness, his low self-esteem. Although never telling Linda his fantasy of her being savior, he solemnly prayed for its consummation. Linda Teixeira came to him as God on a Sunday afternoon.

That Sunday went like this.

After perusing the Zone the night prior, and as most Sundays of late, he rose from his crumbed bed to return to the city. He had two motivations. One would be completed.

The first motivator, exiting the brick house of State Street Station, Leonard walked south on Congress until his fat feet throbbed. At the corner of Franklin Street, he stopped and silently prayed. Please God, help me get there. A cool chill whistled between the buildings of finance and debt. He continued up Franklin and stopped at the corner of Arch Street where guilt beckoned him to attend the first motivator, Catholic Mass. He peered down the quiet street. Men and women sat on folded cardboard beds, holding cup in hand to beg. Parishioners walked by saving their money for the church as their Christianity napped. Please God help me get there, he prayed again at the corner.

Leonard had not been to church, or any other place of worship, since God succumbed to a blood clot on September 20, 1980. Death of his mother, coupled with the propensity to daydream, boredom clipped his mind, and he simply moved on.

He took a left onto Hawley Street and strolled behind Filenes into the black and cold shade. At the corner of Summer Street, sun grazed his handsome face. A man read a newspaper while his Portuguese Water Dog shat on cobblestone patches of lawn. Leonard walked toward the sun, craning like a plant, attempting to deter mental illness.

The second motivator, Leonard ambled uptown pass the banks and vaults where Washington slept. Beyond the Jeweler's Building, where gems lay in fear of abduction, he finally arrived at his destination that sat majestic and inviting like a casino. His head dimly buzzed as his fat feet shimmied through the revolving door where Dostoyevsky and Tolstoy posthumously spoke from the dead. I will read one book a week, he had promised himself months prior. To purchase one book a week was his second motivation. The promise held and he became addicted to books. Upon finishing a novel or simply getting low, he became desperate like a junkie without a bag. He strolled the aisles chatting at the books.

"Hey," he said to Papa Hemmingway.

Further on he pulled up a chair and sat facing the faux wooden shelves. My fuckin' feet, he thought. He fingered the book covers as if brail, stopped at Vonnegut and grimaced. He had a love/hate relationship with Kurt. Leonard so loved, *God Bless You, Mr. Rosewater*, he bought another by the master. While reading *Welcome to the Monkey House*, Leonard's emotions and thoughts ran amuck. He blamed his subsequent wavy mood on the author. Fuckin' feet, and, Fuck you Kurt, ran his mind. Maybe I'll finish my own novel.

Ice Cream Man, 20,983 words, sat in the bottom drawer of his dead mother's wedding bureau. Begun in November, finished in December via bipolar blitz. Sister said she liked it. Cousin did too. A smile placated Leonard's face for a while. However, laziness, the cousin of procrastination, smudged the smile an eraser to chalk. The work lay stagnant entombed in the bureau, a memory like his mother.

Leonard scooted his ass and chair.

"Hi ya," said a perky tin drone.

From high above, Bach orchestrated from unseen speakers. Leonard Turkleton thought he heard an angel and did not look at her when he returned to earth. He waited for, We need that chair, or, You're blocking the aisle. Instead, she stood behind him with a sweet, sweet smile. Waiting. Waiting more. When he did not reply, the aforementioned smile crashed like the recent stock market. Although sensing him some kind of nutbag, she ventured another risk.

"Hey ya," she said.

Leonard finally pivoted and watched the animation. His mind frozen, mouth cement, he watched her lips move as if a cartoon. Head streaked black, white and brown, matched her camouflage pants.

"I've seen you here every Sunday for the last few months. My name is Linda. Listen, I'm not supposed to do this, but do you want to get coffee, or somethin' sometime?"

His head tingled and he thought it might be the blood pressure medicine. Her perfect teeth matched her perfect lips. Her perfect voice. Leonard fought the urge to head for the door. His cognitions fought to survive, and so relied on aggressiveness. I am Caligula, he thought. Kill them.

Leonard stood as quick as he could, extended his fat hand, and felt her softness. *J O H N* inked on her knuckles. He did not ask.

"My name is Turk. Nice to meet you."

"Nice to meet you Turk."

And so it goes. Books no longer lured Leonard to the majestic place beyond the precious stones. They did not suffice.

...ring, ring. Groggy Leonard picked up the receiver to speak to his doll.

" Hello."

Yet out grated the raspy old voice of Ms. McDermott.

"Oh, hello Leonard. Hoped I'd catch you. Could you work some overtime on Saturday, second shift just 'til the patients finish supper?"

His mind raced as he hated his supervisor, The Munchkin.

"Sure," he impulsively replied.

"Excellent. Thank you."

"Sure."

"See you later today."

"Bye."

He placed the receiver in its crown, and pouted it was not Linda. He stumbled to the bathroom and began to piss. He thought of Ms. McDermott and whispered to the wall, Cunt. Midstream of relief, the phone rang again. He tried to finish. "Fuck!"

Leonard finally reached the phone.

"Hello!"

"Hi Baby," she said as she had Monday through Friday for the last three months.

Linda Teixeira sat propped against the side of her undersized bed, a remnant of childhood. Robert Frost read from the current month on the wall. Staring at the sled and snow the poem was penned upon, she spoke to Leonard Turkleton, the man whom she had lost interest. Her fear of being alone incited the call.

The poem hung in the Cape Style house in the City of Lynn, the month left permanent on January. Seven of the boxes were marked Benton. On the cracked window ledge stood three orange bottles, what Linda deemed temporary housing for her pills. She had several diagnoses and the concoction hid them as best they could. At least she could go out. She was adamant never to let Leonard see her off the meds. The primary diagnosis was major depression with suicidal ideation and borderline personality traits. Later bipolar shoveled into the mix. Dr. Benton had different slants and versions, yet mainly kept to these for sake of insurance matters and monetary gains. The good doctor had other motives too. Linda Teixeira, file 12569-06, was simply a sad young woman in a world where happiness was the goal, so said the magazines. The inherited DNA did not agree.

"Hi. I didn't think you were going to call," said now cheery Leonard.

"Of course I was going to call. I called earlier and the phone was busy. Are you cheating on me?" she somewhat chided in the soft voice of black and white movie starlets she once watched with her alcoholic mother.

"Yeah. I mean no. No I'm not cheating on you, and yeah Ms. McDermott called to ask if I would work some overtime."

"When?"

"Saturday night."

"You goin' to?"

"I told her yes. I need the extra money."

A silence lingered. And lingered.

"What's wrong Linda?"

"Oh nothin'."

"No. What?"

"Well, I think it's kinda' strange that we never meet on Saturdays. Sundays you come to see me at the store and the rest of the week is me callin' you to wake you up. We never go out."

"I'm very busy."

However, Leonard's paralyzing fear of public ridicule, solely due to obesity, was truly the reason. This rule of esteem did not apply to Saturday night porn, the only time Leonard drank alcohol.

"Too busy for me? I miss you and I want to see you."

Turkleton felt trapped. The thought of losing Saturdays caused him to panic. The thought of the public panicked him more.

"Leonard, I want you to fuck me again."

And like a switch, he felt powerful.

"Okay, Saturday at six meet me at the wall across from Kelly's," said Caligula.

"Really?"

"Really."

"Alright, get up for work I'll call you tomorrow."

14

Linda Teixeira went back to her soaps. Leonard Turkleton, having agreed to her demands, lost more credibility and interest in the starlet's eyes.

Saturday was a long, long day. It began with a sodium blowout and promissory wink at the restaurant where little roach bastards hid in the dark shade of menus and booths. No porn, and a galloping of sorts around the corner to Stage One. He felt nervous, funny, and shy. Euphoria overcame him as he pushed open the door that divided the dark hallway from the overly bright street. At the start of class, the conman welcomed the students and proceeded showing his portfolio. He then played videos of commercials he had acted in. He spoke of drama, humor, and the craft. Leonard marveled at the professionalism of the conman.

Turkleton met the others. There were two very attractive women. Trina was a singing waitress on a nightly cruise around Boston Harbor. The other, married, what's her name, a student at a local college studying something or the other. Five or six other students, Leonard found so quirky he could not remember them later. Yet, Leonard became more and more euphoric until he felt as if floating. He had no reference, education, or idea that he suffered a mood disorder.

Euphoria remained until passing an alley two hours later. The alley was dark as it had been since 1897 when the third and final wall was erected. Trash and grime nestled, occasionally moving at the vertex of the 90 degree angles. The alley had visitors. Three men lurked beneath the fire escape of the east wall. The men passed a bottle until spotting the intruder. They stared at him in their beaten clothes and leather red faces. The scene, its stage, cast and lighting mesmerized the aspiring actor. The men laughed amongst themselves. It was not guttural, but the camaraderie one senses when listening to an inappropriate sex joke. Leonard awed as he peered at the surrealistic portrait of down and out.

One bum started swaying toward Leonard. He quickly noted that the man he assumed elderly was indeed young. The bum alike Leonard wore camouflage pants. His hair hung long, matted on a heavy denim jacket. Elastic corralled his red beard. In the hot humid air, the man did not sweat.

"Can I help you or somethin'?" the man asked.

Leonard counted four teeth at most in the cavernous mouth full of dark and smoke. The actor imagined hell. The homeless man stared into Leonard's eyes. Leonard stared back at the zombie like animation. Time seemed eternal, an epiphany, a connection for both men. Leonard thought it might be some type of spiritual experience. Then he wondered how even knew that phrase. Maybe it was A.A. many years ago, when a child sitting next to father in the fuckin' halls. Leonard thought of Jesus Christ.

What Leonard perceived as spiritual was actually distorted thinking brought about by his recent depression. Although euphoric at times, he was still depressed. Hypomania allowed Leonard to temporarily step out of the lower affect. Fears that normally caused him to daydream now produced a heightened sense of being. Wondering at the scenario of the alley, Leonard felt someday he might end up there. One day he would be a bum.

A progressed alcoholic at the current age of thirty-three, the man continued staring with distant eyes full of wine and liver disease. The bum did not care about A.A.'s message of hope. He knew himself hopeless. He and his alley pals were leftovers from the 12 Step Program, no matter what A.A. claimed as a success rate.

Leonard's head buzzed and his thoughts raced. Panic entered his psyche. Something told him to move on and he thought it might be a message from God. Surely it could not be his mind causing the self-preserving thought.

"Must be divine intervention," he mumbled to the stale air of the alley.

He quickly pivoted and galloped away leaving the bum to his familiar solitude. After Leonard departed the man posed the question again.

"Can I help you or somethin'?"

He did not know the intruder had left. He did not see the grime and soot of the alley. Moments later he remembered the fuckin' kid. Beyond the wetted brain and soul, he thought the intruder might be another student from Northeastern doing a paper on sociology or the like. Traveling back, he remembered his own stint at a local state college. It seemed such a long time ago when drinking was fun and sleeping with beautiful women was a common occurrence. Such a long time ago. Such a long time ago. Now he wished he could go back and his hazel eyes began to tear. Like his soul, the army green bottle neared empty.

As Leonard strolled down the street, he thought of the man. Although sad, he was glad the man had constituents as they were. He frowned while thinking of old high school pals who had vanished after high school and marriages. In an attempt to shake the blues, Leonard hotfooted for another Chinese restaurant.

Eight black benches attached to four red tables, Leonard sat and gazed out the filmed window at the filmed fairyland. The waiters waited while the cooks cooked. Leonard missed his wink. Chinese singers sang from a crackling tape player out back. Leonard imagined himself Caligula and thought of how he would change this world. He was playing emperor once again. He daydreamed of the bum with hazel eyes and named him James. James Van Brocken III, born in the south just shy of a Tennessee Williams play. James's father was Kurt Vonnegut and was raised in the good ol' Baptist religion and church. Leonard's mind hovered above like a director in a hydraulic chair. A bipolar shift, his affect changed with his current surroundings. The small Chinese waiter in white wore sad eyes. The apparent owner in a satin robe, a wannabe Kung Fu nut, dropped a piece of bread and picked it up on the way back to the operatic kitchen. Slanted Chinese eyes now squinted at Leonard because he was a spy. Anger built slowly and swelled. He traveled beyond the rage and became numb. He was a child again.

Mother put him in the yard so she could clean the house. All quiet except the slapping laundry hanging to dry. A calm wind came in from the marsh. He did not see the marsh rats (Chinese men argued in the distance). Loneliness snuggled between the rays of sun leaving behind a scorched sun. He sighed.

Mother screamed and ran down the old wooden stairs.

"Rah," she yelled. " Rah!"

The boy cried.

Let me see. Stay still, she demanded of the now hysterical boy.

She carried her baby back to the house.

"Puppy," he said, as rats ran into the marsh.

Leonard headed home taking the familiar buses and trains. The bus ride undoubtedly his favorite. It rode by the beach, its smashing waves, and its half-naked women. Wind flew over the beach wall to hit his face hanging out the window. He looked toward the sky and wondered when his God would make him feel better. Better yet, would he? He stared at the ever-changing water and knew it to be more stable than himself.

Arriving home, he lay down on his bed. In the distance a basketball bounced. Its chaotic beat rocked him to sleep. He dreamed of rats.

Hours later, he rose and readied for work. White uniform draped on a chair, then painted on his obesity. To minimize public scrutiny, he walked the long route to the bus stop. He boarded the 411 bus and pretended to sleep so not to look at the virtual and supposed glares. The overwhelming noise of the engine, honks, and chatter, all shunned to a land of distraction. Eyes closed, his mind traveled quicker than the 411.

The nursing home stood as it had the day before, as it had for Leonard's prior four years. Its mauve walls housed the sick and decrepit where many patients made requests and demands. The quiet remained quiet. Leonard feared one patient named Melvin, a man who became resentful after suffering a stroke. The patient sat in his wheelchair or bed, the dayroom or potty, blaming God. A firecracker waiting to explode. After cursing and denouncing his Heavenly Father, in the evening the one sided man would hold a rosary, meditate and pray for salvation. However, in the morning while craving his first cigarette, vulgarity would fly with the occasional bedpan at the orderlies who cared for him. Most days the monstrous rage dissipated by second shift when the rosary beads made their way out of the side table. Nevertheless, twice a week Melvin had to be bathed, for reasons beyond Leonard's comprehension, at night. Although hating his job, Leonard was grateful for the paycheck bought porn, sodium blow and the rest.

Sometimes just before sleep, Leonard thought of Melvin and his frozen dead hand holding beads. He would be brought back to the last time he was in church, September 24, 1980, the morning he nearly collapsed leaving mother's funeral. He remembered how he drifted from the church. And just before sleep he would remember the feelings of empty and hollow, and as much as he tried, he was never able to regain feelings of true love. And off to sleep.

Back at the nursing home, life and anger boiled beneath Leonard's self-pity and despair. He now walked the earth self-destructive waiting for someone to fuck with him. Out of control at the core. The break room door opened and Leonard peered up from his chowder at a self-proclaimed angel.

"And how are we tonight?" asked the nut Charlotte with packet in hand.

"Okay."

"Leonard I barely know you, but I wanted to give you this. "

She passed him the packet.

Welcome to Overeaters Anonymous, it said.

"Please forgive me for saying this, but my Higher Power led me here today. I am in a twelve-step program for compulsive overeaters. I lost thirty-five pounds twelve years ago and never gained it back. Thank God. I wanted to give you this packet that helps explain the program. I know this is forward of me but I know God wants me to do the service. If there is anything you want to talk about, I would be more than happy to oblige. I will see you later, God bless."

The nut said nothing else, smiled like a nut, the smile one dons during religious mania, and departed. Leonard glanced at the pamphlet and anger rose in him. Rage. The rage of one who could kill.

"Cunt," he said to the empty room, for now he hated Charlotte.

He continued to eat, the pace accelerating.

The cool summer breeze came over the wall and grazed Leonard's chest and made his nipples erect. A clam plate in each hand, he sat on the beach wall and waited for Linda to arrive. He placed the food down and stared at the nursing home across the boulevard. Further along the wall he noticed a couple necking. Leonard shut his puffy swelling fat eyes and thanked God for Linda.

When his watched read 6:30 she was a half hour late. He stared at the black ocean and the white jittery streak caused by the quarter moon. If only I could be that serene, he thought, I would be happy. The smell of the tide then awakened him from the dreamy state. The clams turned cold and his emotions caught fire. The crash of waves woke him more. As rage heightened, a bright laser cut him transversely. The blue dented door opened from the green aging car. Out stepped Linda's best friend Tracy. Three other girls giggled in the back seat. The stench of marijuana.

"Come on Leonard get in," she insisted.

"Where is Linda, is she alright?"

"She's at the party."

He did not recollect making plans of going to any party. Rage continued to build.

"What party? She didn't say anything about a party."

"Just get in," the girl said.

"No. I don't want to go to any party. I'm going home."

Leonard waddled toward the bus stop.

"Come on Leonard," Tracy yelled from the distance.

The car screeched away. He turned to watch it depart. Clams being mauled by a huge wily rat, Leonard's fury rose.

Tracy thought of father as the nicotine stench drenched car sped over the Lynn Bridge. The car, a graduation gift from him to transport his baby to Salem State in fall. Yet, in her bureau draw laid the letter from the college denying admission due to bad grades. The summer lagged for Tracey. Fear of telling Father the bad news built. A tapeworm. She turned to pot to deal with the fear. The pot turned to addiction to alleviate itself. While driving along Swampscott Beach, she remembered the sting of his wrath. The time he hid behind the door as she returned late from her junior prom. How he hit her without saying a word. How she lay there crying in her disheveled gown and makeup. How mother continued pretending to sleep. She lit another joint and headed for Marblehead in the clown car of addicts.

A few weeks passed and fear stuck him like reeds of the marsh. I should have gotten in the fuckin' car, he thought at night before sleep and the nasty dreams. Maybe I'd be happy or at least content? But like the moon and tide where rats feed on leftovers, situations are sure to change with time. Most people never change, so Leonard believed.

All seemed worse due to his distortions. Not only did he fear becoming homeless, he had other intrusive thoughts the average person did not. So he thought. He continually checked the gas stove to avoid a fire that would surely kill all the children on the block. The front door, although latched and bolted with a reverberated click, had to be checked again and again. Fear of STDs and the like overwhelmed him. Did I leave the water running? invaded hours later at work. He thought all the time and did not relax.

His biggest obsession was Linda and the night she did not show on the beach. How could she do that to me? No longer did he answer the old phone at the noontime hour. Eventually the ringing stopped. Bitch. He began replaying conversations with her in his head. Like politics, the occasional small squabbles over nothing. How the words droned and squelched like an amateur playing a Stradivarius. Leonard had jags and sprints of self-pity. Even the clerk at Walgreens seemed to be picking on him. All over two cents. He smashed through self-pity and arrived resentful. This turned into weeks.

2:18 a.m., Sunday morning, Linda shows at his door loaded. Tracy egged her on from the blue and green car that never made it to school orientation. And high, Tracy thought of the past.

Tracy's father, John McDermott, a big man, stood above most physically and was a braniac. However, he could not think his way out of his now three-hundred-pound body. One Friday night he waited for his little cherub to walk through the gothic brick entrance of their million-dollar home in Winchester. A friend passed on that his little baby did not go to orientation, but in fact went to work the said day. Sitting in a local coffee shop, John McDermott listened to his buddy cop who happened to be married to a nurse. The nurse worked with Tracey at the hospital in Salem. Somehow the names came up. And so it goes. The giant once again stood in the darkness of the room. The key turned the knob quiet-like. Furious and fists clenched, John McDermott was about to take up boxing, again. His only other opponent never asked for a rematch, and she lay in bed pretending to sleep. Tracey entered the darkness. A sting. A flashbulb blast. She now lay on the floor. She felt the course rug below her cheek. Shame. Degradation. She rose to her feet, legs of a sailor, stared into her father's wet eyes and knew she would be attending school the next semester.

Linda leaned her wet drunken face against the screened door and rang the doorbell. She could taste the metallic rust. Leonard always slept with the door slightly open in case of an imagined fire. His girth slowly came into view out of the darkness. Staggering slowly toward the door, he was frightened by the face hanging on the screen like a leech

"You fuck," she screamed in a slow, loud slur.

He said nothing.

"How the fuck could you tell Tracy's dad about her not going...?" turned, and vomited.

Wine and fries riddled Linda's face, the screen, the porch. Pigeons and marsh rats awoke. She fell to her knees and vomited again.

Leonard shut the inside door and bolted the lock with a clang. He turned and walked down the short hall to the short kitchen. Linda retching beyond his care, he stopped and thought of his onetime hero. Like a defeated prizefighter, Linda Teixeira, now stumbling to the car, no longer held that title.

He sat in the dark kitchen with a bowl of leftover macaroni and reminisced of the past. Remembering Ma, and off to daydream, the food being violently shoveled. He recalled an old apartment, old family and friends. He nodded off in the old decrepit chair. Pigeons returned to sleep as marsh rats scurried for their lukewarm meal.

Autumn then winter dragged. He worked and went home. Worked and went home. On rare occasion, Leonard would visit a relative. They would offer him to stay but he always had to get to work. His insides were corroding and he did not care. He wandered like the men drinking cheap wine from paper bags at Park Street Station. He drifted and surfed life as if a wave of perpetual doom, feeling victim to the universe, or God, or whatever ran this fuckin' place. Yet, somehow, Leonard felt hope. It was not a feeling but a dream, an illusion of sorts. Dreaming, technically daydreaming, had always removed him from the pain. Now he relied upon its reinforcement as he slowly isolated from the world. He'd dream of Ma. Of watching old black and whites movies. Of Richard Widmark. Of Ma smoking Tarrington 100s. Of Engelbert Humperdinck crooning from Mother's old wedding stereo on a weekday after school. Of the spotless home. Of the cat name Quasar. Of being happy.

Acting classes ceased. Simple pleasure like watching football became tedious and mundane. Adventures to the Zone had been limited. Giants and their gigantacisms now replaced by dirty magazines in the library beneath his bed. He binged on carbs and became addicted to its isolation, the only place he felt warm. Leonard drifted ever so slowly along the highway of misery where others were doing time. Now, he habitually noticed loneliness of the infirmed at work. Goodness, positive attitude, gratitude, now suffocated like Melvin in 3B. He drank on weekends off while listening to rock and making love to the women in the library. James Van Brocken III appeared nightly in his dreams and nightmares. Leonard Turkleton was ignorant of the onslaught of depression he suffered. Subsequently, he did not seek help. And Linda was gone for good. Cunt. Upon surpassing 400 lbs., Leonard quit his job and began receiving Social Security Disability Insurance. Habitually sitting, he thought of the future and its futility. Realistic moments became obsolete as each day brought another serving of emptiness. So, so slowly, life had its way and his mind wandered like a nomad.

March 1989

Time and life methodically danced. On a day least expected, Leonard and his obesity met another lover.

Already bored with the confines and despair of unemployment, at the nudge and push of a vocational counselor, Leonard headed out to take a vocational test at the vocational training room, down the hill from the State House at the state run vocational unit. The vocational building with its vocational desks and vocational chairs, ironically seemed vacated. The building, which consumed an entire block, was intended to be a modern day museum. That did not pan. Instead, the south half of the monstrosity was a state run vocational unit, while the north half was a state run mental health facility. What the fuck? Leonard thought. Some state employees entered both ends of the building depending on the time of the year and the current state of their affect.

After testing with #2 pencils, and placing wooden block and pegs in their place, the vocational counselor gave Leonard the results.

"Well Mister Turkleton, your scores in grammar are below average. However, your math skills are very, very, good. Off the charts if you will. After considering the total scores, it is highly suggested that you go into business. Your vocabulary and leadership abilities seem primarily good. Your sentence structure is not. You will be good at management."

Leonard listened to the woman with her insights. He scanned her old shoes and frayed pants, her wild hair and tea stained teeth and judged her. Fuck this, he thought and strode for the state run cafeteria.

Having spent most of his life in a passive state of mind, Leonard decided he would begin to take risks. While eating lunch, avoiding supposed and realistic stares, he scanned the room. A woman mindlessly doing needlepoint smiled at him. And Leonard, having just lost 38 lbs. at the stimulations induced by bowel evacuating milkshakes, felt better about himself. After discarding the lunch tray on the conveyor belt, he trudged the ballroom-sized floor toward the woman's continual smile.

"Hi my name is Leonard. If I give you my number would you call me sometime?" he asked methodic and quick.

Initially unresponsive, she reached in a bag and retrieved a pen. She tore the corner of the paper mat, wrote her number and handed it to him.

She finally spoke, "My name is Renee."

And that is how they met. The beginning of a very brief relationship.

Three days later Leonard borrowed his cousin's little white car and squeezed behind its obtrusive steering wheel. He picked up Renee in her hometown just beyond the whizzing of Route 128. He mentally frowned as she walked toward the car door for she was more homely than he remembered. His obesity dissuaded him from getting her door. They headed for the shores of Rockport. Small talk. Small talk. Small talk.

Snow no longer covered the earth of Rockport but slid back into her dark seas at the dusk time hour. Leonard parked the car horizontal on a patch of grass painted between a dirt road and the frigid ocean. On that cliff, he leaned and kissed her. Vacated summer bungalows and inns, strokes of brown on black canvas, pasted beyond the road. Her beautiful eyes shone nicely. Her bad breathe, as if pieces of breakfast caught in her teeth, filled the car with obnoxious. Leonard did not care if it were acidosis. Nasty is all he thought of its stench.

He ventured beyond the odor and groped the breasts of her plump body. Manipulative and cunning, he moved in such a way in hopes she would notice the bulge in his nylon pants. She grabbed for and rubbed his penis through the static material. Abruptly she stopped.

"I want to go home now," she simply said.

"What the fuck, he simply thought."

Small talk ceased and the wind attempted to sway the little white car out of its prospective lane on 128. What the fuck. What the fuck. Small talk of his mind.

He pulled into the driveway of her home.

"Leonard I had a great time."

"Are you sure?"

"Yeah, I mean, I don't know you well enough to go beyond that for now."

"Oh, he retorted."

"But," and she smiled, " if you take me to the movies sometime I promise to blow you."

What the fuck, his brain now smiled. They kissed goodnight and off into

24

the cold air she took herself and the stench. He dropped the car off at his cousins, placed the keys under the floor mat, and walked back to his house in the city slush.

The next day he called pretending to be a gentleman.

"Hi Leonard. I was hoping you would call."

"Renee I have to be honest with you. I don't think this will work out. I just wanted sex."

She screamed into the phone informing Leonard of his fate to be dealt out by her brother. Leonard Turkleton did not sleep well for the following few nights, peeking often from the confines of a curtained window. He did not know she was an only child.

The remaining of winter passed with the viral of depression a leech on his soul. Now the only refuge left was the dank cold streets of the Zone. It was there Leonard believed the truest portrait of humanity was painted. Hustlers hustled, thriven thrived, others drank and drugged. Choose you weapon, he thought. Chaos for all.

Another Saturday and Turkleton found himself loathing the mundane qualities of masturbation. The Orange Line dropped him off at Tina's reek and up into the streets of heaven and hell. He walked by the rat-infested alleys and ended at the Glass Slipper. He drank expensive/cheap beer and seemingly watered down vodka. Drink up or the barmaid/ dancer/ hooker/ peep show extraordinaire might beckon the doorman to have a chat with ya. Technically, one could have their nose snapped for not drinking like an alcoholic. Leonard left the Slipper and jimmied his fat ass into a booth at the Naked I. After a few there, he scanned the room and wondered if anyone might be Renee's brother. Now courage overcame him.

He exited the bass pounding, pussy dipping stage show, swayed onto Beech Street, and walked half a block. He spotted her at the corner of Harrison between the Chinese bank and restaurant. She just finished a fifteen-dollar handjob in the alley off Tyler. She stood tall, summoning business, flashing her wares. She's the one, Leonard thought. She's the one.

"As pure as the snow covering this hell," he said aloud as he waddled toward her.

"What you want? You surely aint no cop with that beautiful belly jigglin'."

"I like my belly," he said with a grin.

"What else is jigglin' hon?"

"You a cop?" he asked.

"Thirty-five and I'll let you shoot on my perky little titties cuteness," she replied.

He handed over fifty in the alley. She stroked him then took his penis in her mouth. Somewhere between, Starbright, magically produced and applied a condom while rats skittered quietly not giving a shit one way or another. It was over in less than a minute. She was a pro. So was he.

December 1999

Leonard blinked and turned thirty-four. To celebrate, he took his S.S. check and obesity along the same transits and waits back to Tina's reek. All but four dollars for the train and bus he spent on booze, dancers and porn. The pain of depression, entwined with poverty, overwhelmed him. He wandered the cold streets for someone, or something to save him. He sat on the cold slate steps near the Y.M.C.A. and peered across the street at the alley of Head Place. A figure leaned against the east wall of Head Place. In the years frequenting the Zone he could not recall ever seeing this person. Squinting and scrutinizing, he decided the figure to be a women. He remembered his four dollars, stood, and headed for Park Street Station.

3

Benton, 1988

Doctor Benton became irritated not having found the meaning of life. For this quest prompted Jonas James Benton to study, train, then practice in the field of psychiatry. Initially the goal was to be a surgeon. However, on one autumn day a famed neuropsychiatrist visited Harvard to preach of cognitions, their distortions, relevancies, irrelevancies, and finally their potentialities. Benton sat in on this lecture during his third year of med school and it changed his life long goals. Liver disease and such were boring in comparison to dialectic and behavioral studies. Immediately following Harvard Medical School, Benton secured an internship at a celebrated nuthouse just west of Boston. And on these solemn grounds, one patient changed his life.

At the conclusion of their very first session, Belinda Tremonte wheeled back around on her yellow fuck me pump stilettos before exiting the room.

"Everything is fate," she said stern and quick through frosty painted lips. "We have absolutely no say in the matter."

Belinda departed as quickly as she spoke. Once the old maple door closed, Dr. Benton held his head in hands sensing the inevitable that may occur. He sat back in the creaking chair, unzipped his pants, and began to masturbate. When done, he cleaned himself. An oncoming migraine caused temple veins to bulge like the waters of the nearby Merrimack River as Benton sat in a state of panic. Why did I choose psychiatry? He rose, moved the chair over to the window, and opened it to air out the room. He sat and laid his head on the cold sill. Dreaming permeated his synapses; he drifted and recalled moments of adolescents.

Fourteen years old and the family had once again settled into their summer home on a pristine lake in New Hampshire. Father threw parties for days. Beyond cheers and jeers of these memorable events at the Big House, the prestigious guests eventually went on their way, a handshake, a hug, having never liked Jerry Benton to begin with. They only showed to kiss ass with the State Rep.

From old money, which new money people liked, Grandfather Benton was indeed the main attraction. Most confided in the ancient man adorning a precisely trimmed beard, dangling, willow tree eyebrows, and the propensity to quote the Massachusetts General Laws Annotated, Freud's works on the super-ego, and the Catholic and King James versions of Bible. In a room of men after a few Scotches, he could also cite the Marquis de Sade. His wallet always bulged with the said old money and his lineage stepped off the Mayflower. He semi-privately believed himself superior in race. Most loved Grandfather Benton for his loving heart and philanthropy wallet. For reasons unbeknownst to most, his wife shunned her husband at times in public. And this held true in their bedroom, with its twin beds, twin nightlights, and twin miseries. Secretly, counting his wife, a handful of no-names and the one time blackmailer, Grandfather Benton was a misogynist.

Therefore, the old man loved Jonas more than the stars and heaven, and the beloved stocks and bonds that made him rich. Although used only by Papa, "Little John," or, "Jon Jon," became the nickname bestowed at the baby's christening. A gleam arrested their eyes whenever they met. The mere hint of Papa's cigar would stifle the boy's shyness and bring out a clown, a soldier, an adventurer. The room they inhabited became a Big Top, battlefield, at times Heaven. Papa would light up the big brown stick, as Grandmother called them, and the boy would melt into pride. The pride of Spartacus. The boy sat for hours while the man read books by Twain, Dostoyevsky, from Genesis to Christ. The old man's patch of gray-red hair, flaming waves, sat near the stoked fireplace reflecting a godlike symbol to the boy.

All the while, resentment festered within Jerry Benton for the favoritism shone upon his son. The little bastard, he would mumble of the boy during solitude walks in the woods. During this one particular summer, the agitated congressman made a grave mistake.

Benton found the dirty magazine the neighboring Kahn boys left in the woods, Twenty yards northwest of the old oak, just beyond the path, Johnny Kahn had informed. Thumbing through it like a mad scientist, the pubescent Benton felt an adolescent twinge in the groin and its subsequent Catholic guilt. However, like most his age, Benton did not care.

As he thumbed the pages, Mother yelled for the boy to come to dinner. When her caterwauling did not cease, Jerry looked for his son. Rage the chaser to his four mixed drinks, he crossed the back lawn and ambled into the woods. At the bank of a creek, he stumbled and fell into its muck. Fury rose like Christ's third day.

The younger Benton became frightened upon hearing snapping of twigs in the dark thicket of woods. The boy froze as the beast emerged. The beast smiled the smile of one buying a house or car. The boy froze as if one in the presence of a grizzly. Father walked toward son as if climbing the State House stairs, white shirt, silk tie.

"Hi Dad."

Father spotted the dirty magazine now wedged between the rock and tree just beyond the boy's sneaker feet. The man's smile gone. How could my son do this to me? he self-righteously thought. Fourteen years expecting perfection from the boy seemingly smashed to its respective delusion. Without warning, prior offense, intent or threat of such action, the man hit Benton with such force, the boy and gravity traveled parallel to the dirt of God's good earth. The hunter now stood confused above the bird with the broken wing, for it did not cry or wince. It was not the forceful blow, nor the unjust justice served, the venial offense was the dishing out of shame. Jerry loomed above his prey with eyes of a killer. Years of resentment a tick on his back. Hatred, malevolently danced as the boy would not cry. And the distortion of perfection etched into the boys mind.

"And furthermore, not a word to your mother."

Benton rose from the cold sill and stared out the window at the trees of the famed nuthouse, its calmness and quiet, then shut his eyes again.

Back in the darkness of forest, Benton awakened to the harsh reality of violence. The Bentons stared each other down knowing a line had been passed. Like the time the boy swam beyond the sectioning rope at the lake. In the nuclei of thicket of darkness, fear, shame and love intermingled under the whitening stars and the heavens took note, Jonas Little Jon Benton lost respect for the hunter. And Father felt nothing, for alcohol had done its job.

Perfection, ah perfection, lingered in the boy throughout the summer and beyond. He became freaky about germs, God, religion, Satan, diseases and girls, etc., etc... Anything that could ruminate in the mind did. These obsessions with perfection drained the already anxious boy. School is difficult when one has to achieve an A+. Perfect health is trying when another does not cover their deadly cough. No longer did he need Father's expectation of perfection. He could tend to that himself.

Benton awoke from the coldness of daydream and sill, dragged the chair to the desk and sat. He opened the first drawer and retrieved a bottle of pills.

29

He opened the second drawer and retrieved a bottle of Scotch. He swallowed four pills with drink. He did not open the third drawer for the contents within separated this world from the next. The painkiller kicked, he shut the drawers and headed home.

The earlier life of Benton; prestigious places

Adolescence passed and Benton achieved all goals Father had set pardoning perfection itself. The seed of Jerry eventually realized the insanity of its quest. However, he still clung to some routines instilled in him as a child. Performing military workouts, making military beds, he followed suit of his onetime military Father. Insult to injury, Jerry Benton had never seen a battle, conflict, or skirmish. As Vietnam was killing, Jerry laid on a Hawaiian beach when not writing letters for his Colonel. The younger Benton followed once again. After high school he enlisted, was sent to Indonesia, wrote letters for a General. Lacking war and skirmish, the only conflict within Benton secretively lay in his swaying sexual preference. And alcohol did its job.

A letter.

Dear Mr. Jon James Benton, the Fellows at Harvard would like to extend an invitation to you this Fall 1978 session. Please let us know at a suitable time. If we do not hear from you by August 3, 1978, we will consider you having passed, at which time we extend our best wishes. The Deans.

The shivering plane flew over Jakarta headed for Boston. Benton looked down at her jungles and dropped a tear onto its green memory.

Following a small town parade for his service, Grandfather honored Benton by throwing a party. He pulled the soldier aside and made him sit in the library of the Big House. Cigars plumed as the old man slipped Benton a check for $200,000.

"A little spending money Jon Jon."

Outside the clouded window, Jerry played horseshoes with the likes that kissed ass. He peered into the room, its cigars, its money, its love, and felt desperation. Benton packed the following day and headed for his first prestigious place.

How he really acquired admission

Jerry Benton's perfectionism paid off in the 70s when he secured the Administrator position at an acclaimed hospital in Boston. Sure he kissed ass a bit, but graduating summa cum laude at the famed Wheaton College of Business will get you places. Along with the rocketed paying job came the perks. He met lucrative people in the business, medical, art, entertainment and sports worlds. In times of desperation, say as when a loved one is seriously close to death, Administrator Benton was a good ally to have if one needed a favor. One pimply back washed another.

Enter C.E.O. Peter Champlain, III, the brain, back and determination of an established funding house in the city's financial district. He entered Jerry's office wearing a three-thousand-dollar suit, and million-dollar shit-eatin' grin. The pair faced one another, father figures in a G.Q. snapshot.

"Peter me boy, how are you?"

"Jer', what happened Saturday? I had to tee off with the likes of the Conrad boy. I thought I needed a shrink."

"Well maybe you do. Would you like me to call downstairs and have one come up?" the Administrator asked the C.E.O.

Florida faces stretched and laughs abound in sinister cackle as the two talked golf, President Reagan, and golf. Instantly the proverbial poker face adorned the C.E.O.'s face and demeanor. Business about to begin.

"I was surprised to get your urgent call Peter, what's going on?"

"I need a favor," said the C.E.O. "I had this twit flying in from San Diego to give my company a motivational kick in the ass type speech. Well, to cut to the chase, the fucker cancelled. Has the flu or some shit like that."

The Administrator sat with fingers and thumbs connected in the shape of a triangle. He tapped the indexes of the triad to his forehead as if pointing a gun or wishing away a migraine. His beady slit eyes stared down the adversary. The room, a business place where survival of the least is sure to be trampled. Seldom is a place, as men partner to build Ivy walls, and skyscrapers reached for the moon, there a sense of goodwill or kinship. A place where men live just below humanity and scratch one another like rats. And if one arrives at the top of the heap of fecal matter, does he or she ever find it enough. He or she then wants to be a god. Falling short, they administrate to others in supreme mode, at times they fall hard, end in mother's arms, or become nomads of an alley.

"So how can I help?" asked the Administrator.

"Might you do twenty minutes of motivating this Thursday night using your twisted wasp humor?" said the olive suit.

Jerry smirked and pushed the button that wired through the soundproof walls to summon Jennifer.

"Yes Mister Benton?"

"Jen cancel everything I have this Thursday from three on. Dinner reservations for two at the Parker House. And tell Thomas I will need him and the black Lincoln for the night until two or three."

"Yes Mister B.," she responded sweet and slow like one of his high paid escorts. She did not ask if Mrs. B. would be attending.

"Thanks Jer', you're the best. Now I can sleep again. How's the boy?"

The Administrator leaned back in the leather womb. The triad now resting on his belly, he subtly countered.

"Well," said Jerry.

"What's wrong B., is he sick?"

"No, no. The little bastard applied for Harvard Business and was rejected. He barely had the grades and didn't have enough extracurricular. An Associate Dean stated he lacked enthusiasm."

"No fuck," said the C.E.O.

Cars passed like snakes on the winding Storrow Drive below. People walked like anemia to their dreaded place. The C.E.O. stood staring across the Charles River at Harvard and M.I.T.

"Don't say another word," said the olive suit, sat its olive ass on Jerry's desk and made a call.

Gerald Benton, the first, sat quietly in wait. To pass the moment he fucked Jen, again, in his mind.

"Ivy League it will be," said the C.E.O. to the Administrator.

Harvard

Benton was a young lad hanging with the likes of Paul Delaney and the McKay Brothers in the pit of Harvard Square, yet, he never passed through the arches of the prestigious university just across Mass Ave. He remembered gazing across at the infamous yard beyond the stone walls and iron gates. It was not until the very first day of school that Benton finally stood upon Harvard's grounds.

Humming the Beatle's *In My Life*, Benton felt on top of the world. He did not end up at Wheaton. Nor, did he reenlist after a weekend of drinking with Paul Delaney at the Purple Shamrock. No, he was at Harvard. Finally, Father's reins had been snipped like a doped up cat. Congruently, Benton sensed a quaint feeling of doom. As if lightning would strike on a clear summer day, negativity lurked in the not so far reaches of the mind. However, in the same moments he could discern and prioritize. Fundamentally aware, he knew good grades and a low-key existence would sail him through the next four years. He laid on the autumn lawn, sprinkles of red, yellow, gold and orange, the smell of trees and crisp air caressing his face. Beyond Father's reach, Heaven Benton decided this place to be. And just over there was the honking of cars.

Seasons flew like storms and sun. Professors aged slowly like the bus centipedes edging their routes. The first two years were a breeze due to Benton's epiphany to medicine. This occurred after a heated debate during freshman year. Father and son argued about nothing on a bench in Harvard Yard. Benton had enough of Jerry and decided to mentally punch back. No longer would the business track do, or still truer said, Fuck you Dad. Jon James Benton reached for medicine to remedy his soul so switched majors for the sophomore year. And medicine enmeshed nicely with the young Benton.

Grandfather often visited on Sundays to stroll along the Charles with his golden boy. Each time they parted, Benton felt stronger and more motivated in his academic goals. Grandfather was a great talker having wooed the best in the business world and bringing many a whore to a sentimental tear. Father kept his distance except for national holidays that included the consumption of some type of oversized foul or pig. The perfectionist neither coached, nor patted his son's back. Benton focused on Papa, the scent of cigar, the glee, the love, and secretively in the same moments, the inheritance.

Junior Year

Usual and consistent with the load of pre-med, Benton lived the existence of a troglodyte. He meticulously planned and scrimmaged travels between his cavernous dorm room and classes into precise routine. The room was plain and simple reeking dork, geek, boring. Now the bed was never made. The Steve Miller Band hung on the right wall, Grey's Anatomy on the left, the cosmos taped to the ceiling. A lone window peered out the 12 x 8 room at the small backyard and rows of ancient homes full of ancient money. Science books aligned the baseboards of the tiny room, having seen their classes, never to be used again. An old bureau housed all of his clothing except for his wrinkled shirts that hung in the tiny closet behind the tiny entrance door. Pictures of Mother and Father dueling in a duel picture frame. Papa stood tall in a pewter frame, serious, Freud with a slight smile. Meme hid behind him peeking around as if caught in a scandal. Pens, pencils, note pads, more books, and an awkward loneliness set in once he escaped Father's restrictive tentacles.

One Sunday morning after several hours of writing papers, Benton rode his bicycle across the city to the Aku-Aku Restaurant at Fresh Pond. The rackety three-speed climbed the small bridge over the train tracks, sped down its hill and glided the remaining way to the restaurant parking lot. He locked the bike and followed the Pork Lo Mein.

He sat alone in a booth sipping egg drop soup and licking duck sauce off a spoon. Nonchalantly, he glanced across the near vacant room to notice an apparition, so he thought. Her hair platinum blonde, her face pale white like the upside down teacups throughout the place, the apparition was reading. Benton became excited since reading was one of his passions. Red toenails squirmed and shifted amongst each other in leather sandals, her eyes remaining transfixed upon the book. Benton needed to know who she was.

Now shyness stepped aside like the waiter at the restaurant door, letting through the man who needed more than family and books. Benton rose from his sticky plate and sweating bowl leaving ten dollars in its wake. Awkwardly, yet possessing a newfound confidence, he sauntered across the room. Red sneakers torpedoed for the red nails target. Benton knew it was the crossing, the getting across the room, most difficult. He shut out the mind and achieved motivation. Arriving at her booth, below the platinum streaks, the shaved eyebrows and sparkle glittered cheeks, he noticed the apex of an amateur tattoo, jailhouse in color, blurry like speech.

Cautious and slow, "Hi my name is Benton, I mean Jonas, Jonas Benton," and extended his hand as if meeting a banker.

"My name is busy, what do you want?"

Benton's blurriness somehow sharpened and his confidence heightened by the challenge and loathing of rudeness.

"What are you reading?" he inquired more steadily.

She waited a few moments then replied, "Tolstoy's *War and Peace.*" She held the book up for him to see.

"That is one of my favorites," he lied.

A brief silence lingered, little clanking noises off in the kitchen, waiters watched silently from the bar to make sure she was not being harassed.

"Would you like to join me?" she said.

They talked books, Chinese food, art school and Harvard. When the last subject arose, she quickly estimated him not to be a loser, became jovial and flirtatious.

Egg roll tumbling in mouth, she stated, "My favorite is *The Death of Ivan Ilyich* by Tolstoy."

And Benton fell in love.

Their bikes peddled away like a minute quickened parade. Benton led, Clarissa followed as if to catch or earn something from the newest man in her life. After securing the pair of bikes to the rack outside the dorm, they entered the ancient building. Each felt the excitement of mystery. He more than her.

Upon entering the small room, they did not speak for a short while. Clarissa strode toward the small bookcase hugged by the east corner of the room. She softly ran her fingers across the likes of Vonnegut, Nabokov, Dostoyevsky, Kafka, Burgess, Salinger, and Vollmann as if they were once lovers. Her then puffy eyes began to tear. Benton did not witness this until she turned toward him. She walked two paces, shoved him onto the bed that creaked its loud creak. She fumbled for his buckle, button and zipper, pulled the jeans down to his ankles and straddled him. He thought it strange and intriguing that she wore no panties. His mind traveled fast like her gyrating hips. Her semi-Asian eyes added to the mystery. Not long, the squeaking stopped. She dismounted her ride, crashed onto the mattress and the bed's orchestral end. Clarissa lay into his sweaty arm and chest, her wet white back spooned by the old beige wall. They slept.

Benton had a dream. A Sunday way into the future

Coffee, eggs, bacon and pine trees woke him. He was smiling. A note on the kitchen table, Took the kids to the park. Back in a few hours. He ate and smiled, and smiled.

A wind slightly rustled the trees in the yard. Torrential rain followed. Tint flashes and cracks of thunder. Lightning beyond the valley. Panic enraptured the wedded Benton. He rose from the new furniture and headed for the park. Clouds blackened. The car stalled, and stalled, and stalled. Terror consumed him.

Benton woke sweating like the spoon of a junkie. He sat up in the drench to find Clarissa getting dressed.

"Are you leaving now? You can stay the night."

"My business is done here," she responded. "I usually charge fifty, but since I stayed quite a while, and since you seem to have it, it will be one-hundred."

Numb, just shy of surreal, his eyes transfixed on her still naked back, a hunter with site on its prey, resentment seethed and became him. Rage flooded his mind and evil contorted his face. And she witnessed this. However, no concern arose having seen it all before. Benton never felt so humiliated except that time in the woods with Father. Yet, Jonas was a rational, scientific man and personality.

"There is money in the second drawer of the bureau. Only take the hundred."

His head tingled, fists balled, knuckles whitened. A vague wetness, makeup for his lashes, shined in the lamped illumination. He studied her in a room of a hundred shades and hues. Below her left bicep, at the crux of the upper and lower arm, an abscess. Benton hadn't noticed this earlier in the evening when her skin was silky, giving, loving, when he entered her wetted softness and found her womanly place immaculate. Now fear filled the third-year Harvard man as he deduced Clarissa to a junkie.

She walked softly toward him and kissed his forehead. Five twenties clutched in her now boney hand, the junkie turned and opened the door that

36

led to the amber lit hallway.

Clarissa turned back to the exhausted john who had not a word to say.

"Thanks baby," and departed.

His mind spun round like the Ferris Wheel at Paragon Park as a child with Papa. Not knowing what to do and knowing something had to be done, Benton impulsively rose, threw on a robe and socks. He slipped out into the chilled air of night. The ground frosted, he followed her tracks at a quickened pace not caring whether he slipped.

Just inside the gate of the famous yard, he bellowed loudly, "Clarissa!"

She stopped and turned in her bunny tracks. The panicked young Benton ran across the green and white patch of lawn and came upon her.

"What is it Jon?"

"I, I, I want to see you again if it's alright?"

"Of course Sweetie," she replied, shaking not from inclement weather but the gnawing teeth of withdrawal that raked her spine.

"When?" he insisted.

"Meet me at the restaurant our usual time, for dumplings.'

Tears dissipated as did the rage and craze. Benton fell in love again and did not notice his cold feet.

During the following two semesters, they habitually met every Saturday night at the Aku-Aku, only interrupted by holidays, or if Clarissa was secretively in rehab, or, as she put it, "Seein' friends." He always paid for dinner and drinks. Occasionally they met at his grotto when there was a big paper to write or the weatherman got it wrong. For Benton it was sex with a warped twist of love. For her it was another fistful of money to buy clothes in Harvard Square, coffee at Luberto's, cop a few bags. And of course, the money for dope cut first like a dealer sampling the first shards of crystals.

Then the day came when only a week stood between him and his Bachelor's Degree. A Thursday night, Benton insisted on seeing her at an allocated time. He followed her directions and pedaled the ratchet bike to the outskirts of Davis Square in Somerville. They ate at Redbone's then returned to her apartment, a place he'd never been.

They climbed three flights and entered her current home. It was larger than his was and had an uncanny, poor person's minimalism. Along one wall stretched a long metal bookshelf. Benton went to it and smiled having found authors he had, and had not read. Also, Tolstoy, Tolstoy, Tolstoy. Thomas Mann. Burrows. *A Tree Grows in Brooklyn*. Stacks of *National Geographic*. Sinclair. Books on women's rights. Paglia. A book on women and the sex industry. Benton smirked.

He turned and noticed that look in her eye, lust; the crave for sex, money and dope. Benton made love to her. She had sex. They finally laid side-to-side huffing small amounts of air to slow their pounding chests. Benton rolled off the bed onto his knees. Clarissa thought he found religion, or the like, and would soon espouse Armageddon or theories on fucked up evolution. Worse, confess about some type, form, or level of sexual disease. He reached into his accordion pants that lay on the hardwood floor. He pulled out a small black box, opened it, said not a word, and waited patiently for her response. Neither said a word. Passing cars, buses, a delivery man hollering from the street at someone, something, something or another, invaded the quietness of the deafened room.

White noise.

"Clarissa I love you more than I love anything in this world, the heavens, the universe. Will you marry me?"

The ring dimly shined in the late afternoon light that ray through the naked window. Clarissa started to cry. Sobbed. Benton thought this to be good, for he had watched many black and white movies with Papa.

"I, I, I can't Jon. I am not in love with you." Snot drizzled her face and hand.

Time, light, quietness lingered. Benton slowly raised, head fuzzy, fist clenched. He turned from her, sat on the bed and dressed.

He walked out the door quietly mumbling, "Cunt."

Nearing top of his class, Benton graduated and Harvard duly accepted him into Medical School. Three years of med flew quickly as life does for most and Benton found this time enjoyable. He reveled in the long shift at the hospitals, the paperwork, and reporting to superiors. Benton, turns out, was becoming a fantastic man of medicine. Others looked to him for help including physicians themselves. Most found him to be a whiz. Occasionally during moments of trauma, a sweating emergency room doctor would put ego aside and ask the scraggily kid what to do. He obtained, and kept secretive, a gift passed from Grandfather; photographic memory. The ability to retain everything he read came in handy when diagnosing a patient. He remembered all their labs and charts. And one day Benton made a decision that would alter his life forever. He chose to focus in psychiatry.

An internship at a renowned nuthouse west of Boston where three hundred year old trees called depressed patients to lynch themselves, patients and staff loved, "Call me Jon," for he also inherited Papa's humor. He passed the state medical exam during the second autumn at the acclaimed nuthouse. Securing Chief Assistant Psychiatrist of the P.T.S.D. Outpatient Clinic, Benton wore a semblance of contentment on a wrinkle free face. He moved his small medical library into a small office that approximated the size of the old dorm room. Upon receiving his first paycheck, he rented a room just outside of Watertown Square. He drove Father's old Subaru back and forth to work and play.

Then, as the last of the leaves had fallen, and clouds of winter's despair hovered the grayed skies, Benton felt a slight pressure of sorts in his head. Gradually he sensed the mood change and found himself stuck in negativity and sarcasm. Road rage was a common occurrence. As leaves fell from branches that called to the sick, so did his sense of identity fall from the self. One ethical and moral mistake, a moment in time, Benton's life withered with the leaves.

A coal chalk day, frost begging to ice, children lacing their skates for the upcoming week, Benton traveled the famed tunnels of the nuthouse. He climbed two flights of stairs to his office where the beloved books sat so still. So still in the cubicle of mental conditioning. He sat mindful of the quietness, the occasional wind, the gnawing void inside. Aware of his own depression, or a prolonged severity of dysthymia, he refused to call in sick because eight patients were scheduled that day. "Give back to humanity," Papa whispered inside his pressured head. Benton sat in the pseudo-leather chair and felt nothing.

He rose and laid his coat over a wooden chair in the corner. No hooks on the walls for patient's sake, he placed his scarf on top of the long mauve filing cabinet. He sat again and laid his eight o'clock shadow to his chest. He breathed in wearily, cognitive of opioids he could cop.

"What am I doing here? "

He looked upward to what he perceived to be God, Heaven, the hereafter.

Quietness lingered.

Quietness lingered.

A loud rap on the mahogany door disrupted the quiet. Fuck, one of the borderlines late for the 9 o'clock appointment. He opened the door and welcomed Belinda for the third time in two weeks.

"What's up Doc?" she said quick, eyes focused at the floor.

"Still trying to help people," he answered. "Please, sit," motioning his hand to the chair opposite the desk.

Her wet eyes never seeing the inviting hand, she replied, "I would rather stand for a while."

"Okay."

Benton sat behind the desk while Belinda continued to stare at the old rug.

"I cut myself again this past weekend."

"Oh?" he responded, faintly shutting his eyes and nodding his head.

"I want to show you this time, okay?" she asked with sense of urgency. Unblinking eyes now peered at him.

Procedurally to maintain a professional environment he would and should have said no, however, in this time of depression his wits were not right, as if one driving under the influence of an intoxicant.

"Sure," he replied.

She unfastened the long black raincoat. It fell to the floor and surrounded her expensive black boots. His eyes widened so slight. Pardoning her booted legs and feet, she stood naked, a scar transverse the collarbone to left nipple. Raw still. Her wet eyes remained fixed and unblinking. Protocol for the physician in this particular situation is to dial 222. This would expedite a swamp of counselors, nuthouse police, and anyone in the vicinity wearing a nuthouse badge, to respond to the emergency. Benton did not follow protocol. Time hung like spiders behind bookshelves, mites on lampshades. The doctor concave like the borderline personality feet away, dead like ice on a pond, the gluttonous virtue of intrigue swallowed his mind like a shock treatment seizure.

A man induced with loss of control, he rose and walked toward her. Without suggestion, hint, or demand, she bent over and folded her arms on the chair. Her preemptively ready, he unzipped and quickly entered, parting her lips and delusions of trust. No force, groping or attempt at drama. Forget kisses. When done, the room reeked of bleach. He wiped himself off with the knitted scarf and threw it on the floor. Belinda put on her coat. They returned to their prospective chair. Doped up, sexed up, fucked up, she felt numbness and a vague wave of titillation. Benton felt confused and an oncoming dose of panic. Nearing whisper, "I don't think people have a say in their lives. I think it's all destiny."

"Is that so?" he replied.

Belinda had a brief cry, rose, arranged her coat and departed closing the door with a bit of slam. The ethic drained doctor sat in his doom. He stood, picked up the scarf and placed it in the cabinet. He walked to the door and invited in the 10 o'clock.

Mid afternoon, he received an email from his superior Dr. Harold Reinsworth.

The following morning Benton sat in Reinsworth's office. Also attending, Margaret the previous day's 10 o'clock borderline. She again relayed the primal act heard from the waiting area the day prior. Benton did not deny nor defend the allegations as a pelting of guilt had him tongue-tied. After being guaranteed a life of free care at the nuthouse, a scholarship if you will, Margaret, Maggie, Mag, Magoo, became insatiably, financially, and antisocially content. The patient departed leaving the men in the room reeking of Freud.

"I highly suggest, no, I insist that you resign today. That you write a brief letter, pack and leave."

Benton numb, confused, depressed, slowly nodded and left.

Jerry Benton received the call early next day.

"Sorry Jerry, I had to let the kid go."

The deflated father thanked the chum for not letting the issue rise to scandal or suit. He hung up the scuffed red phone and lay back on the bed.

"Who was it?" inquired blindfolded wife.

"No one. Just one of my good chums."

He sat up, slipped into slippers, walked to the library and sat in the big leather chair. He shut his eyes and pondered for a while. He rose and went to the bookshelves, removed Birds of the World, and retrieved the container behind it. He sat again, had a few moments of contemplation, and then a decision. Jerry Benton proceeded to drink heavily for the first time in several years.

Thirty-one years of age and Benton hid from his father. He rented a sleazy hotel room on the outskirts of Boston's Theatre District, formerly known as the Combat Zone. For days, give or take a week, he binged on barleycorn and popped opioids. Amazingly, he was able to pick up the old black phone and call old classmates about potential job openings in the area hospitals. The wear of isolation became too much.

During the second month in the stench-drenched place, Benton paid a hooker seven hundred dollars to work a twelve-hour shift. He pounded the junkie while pondering Clarissa.

The next morning he packed, paid the rent, and left the rodent infested walls of the hotel. He asked Joey at the desk to call a taxi. Waiting outside the establishment of reek, Benton noticed Tinkerbelle across the street at the mouth of an alley. He began walking toward her to wish her well. A car pulled to the curb in front of the whore and a man got out.

"Where is it?" is all Benton discerned in the city's early morning bustle.

The man smashed his bitch in the face for coming up short on something or another. Benton pivoted and strolled back to his respective curb, respective place, and his respective, 'Mind your own fuckin' business." He retrieved the taxi and headed to his next place of employment. The plane was leaving in an hour.

Ohio

Irony. Benton spent the next three years as a rehab counselor in Nowheresville, Ohio. He called home at Christmas for brief chats with Mother and Father. He was too ashamed to speak to Papa. After numerous attempts to keep a semblance of communication, the family eventually stopped trying to contact him. Benton chatted to cows and cornfields on long drives to work.

Meanwhile, Grandfather lost his wits and lay supine, near comatose, in a Wellesley Hills nursing home for the rich. Belinda and Margaret now skeletons collecting dust. Benton deemed Black Sheep by, and of, the family. At unsuspecting times, repressed as Freud predicted, Father would enter his mind. His jaw would clench symptomatic of the congruent migraine, and the pain mimicked that sustained in the midst of the woods. Such a long time ago. Such a long time ago. Phantom limb of the mentally ill.

After brief self-detox, remaining clean and sober since, Jonas James Benton, M.D. specialized in addictions. Due to his fear of euphoric recall to narcotics, he seldom prescribed medicines and became more of a counselor than a doctor. His small windowless office situated at the end of a basement hall, this grotto continuously stank of turpentine due to painters always painting. The hallway aligned with furniture presented four shuffling decades. Cheap paintings produced by patients during their stay or stays. Interior landscape proving fruitful enough to make the healthy depressed, let alone addicts a day, or two, or three from the wasteland of their chosen disease or diseases.

Benton kept no friends. After work he ate all forms and variations of sugar and read voraciously into the night. He often went to the porn drive-in three counties away, his collar high, his hat low. Once every month or so he kept company with a hooker who advertised in a local paper as an escort service. After several times escorted, Benton thought himself in love with Ginger. He told her so. The scarred black woman did not care to hear of it and went back to her pipe. Benton never saw her again. Months later, the local paper told of her demise. Another john became raging after being shortchanged. The disgruntled schoolteacher killed her with an unidentified object. During moments of craze, he dumped her in a cornfield like manure. This scared the crows for a while then they had their peck. A farmer driven tractor shredded the remains of carcass. Some pieces were bagged and made their way to the coroner.

And time dragged.

Benton considered suicide or picking up and knew both to be the same. One drizzling Ohio morning, scarecrows shivered by wind, a secretary secured a note to the corkboard on his office door. He arrived at work and read the note. Call your mother a.s.a.p. He called Weston hoping Father had a premature death. Brutal. Driving back to his apartment Benton stared out the window at Ohio's weathered boredom and silently cursed the gods for letting him down. He pulled the car to the roadside upsetting the dirt's isolation.

He wept violently and screamed, "Papa."

Benton sobbed knowing it was his last days in the Buckeye State.

Boston

Doctor Benton felt pressure in his head as the plane halted on the cement carpet of Logan Airport. During self-reflection, he pegged the time of year as culprit. He tried to shake it off. He stood fatigued waiting at the luggage carousel with the other weary travelers, their pain in the ass kids.

"Fucking bastards," he mumbled.

He splashed water on his face in the plastic smelling restroom, peered into the mirror to notice an adult. He winced. A homeless man sat in the corner near the radiator and stared at Benton. The man smiled and begged for a dollar. Benton snarled in disgust and walked out slamming the door against the tiled wall.

Outside the terminal cabbies sat in their cars and despair reading the daily paper. A black suited man held a sign, Benton Party. Wearied Benton entered the Lincoln.

"Nice to have you home Mister Benton," the black suit said politely.

Benton nodded at the man whose name he had forgotten.

The Lincoln glided along Storrow Drive. Benton gazed across the brown river at the science buildings of M.I.T. He daydreamed in the style of, What would have become of my life if I just...? Chemist versed Doctor, Engineer versed Shrink. Memories of his old Alma Mater brought on a deeper level of aloneness.

Weston

The house painted since his last visit, Benton thought it looked better than he did. Mother stood in the doorway and watched her son get out of the car. She noticed his newfound girth as if an imposter squatted her homestead. Benton walked up the way to Barbara Stanwyck's, Virginia Barkley feet from a shotgun. A hug of sorts, pats and smiles. Polite hellos. Faint quiet and chill in the air like a far off wood burning stove. Benton knew it would be like this since Papa was gone. Mother, like Father, had her own emotional accoutrements that filled ears of shrinks over the span of decades. Moreover, her gut sank knowing her son to be a psychiatrist. The feeling of contempt.

House semi-full, semi-empty of guest, many had come to grieve, to help the grieving, and to kiss ass. It was fashionable for relatives and friends to bring food to the bereaved home so they did. Father sat alone in the game room nursing a drink. Benton put his bags in the room on the second floor and went down to Father who had just lit a cigar.

"Hey Dad."

"Son."

"You alright?"

"Why not? Sure. Want a cigar?"

"No thanks."

"How's it going in cornflake world?" the beginnings of alcohol induced slur.

"Okay," Benton said in low pitch.

"Want a drink?" Jerry asked with a smirk.

"No."

Jabber continued in the room used mostly for that. Rarely did one pretend to play. Benton was surprised when Father reached for a cue stick. He did not know if it were an invitation to play or a warning to suddenly duck.

"Well rack'em up boy. Watch what your father can do to the ego in ten minutes or less."

A short silence. The clacking of balls.

"Is that the goal dad?"

"What's that?"

"To chide me through a measly game?"

Jerry tilted his head upward and stared into nothingness. The eyes of a drunk, drunk once again. Resentments, angers, pities, aggressions, mixed with drinks.

"Well, about the time I...when I hit you. I am sorry."

"I don't want an apology," said the boy.

"Well what the fuck do you want?"

Benton gazed at the west wall where the family hung meticulous in gold plated frames. He then peered at the east wall where an oil of Papa watched the scene. Benton returned his cue stick to the rack and relied on good old sarcasm.

"Father I have to go. You'll have to play with yourself."

He left the room to search for the matriarch of the "big fuckin' mess," the frantic demeanor of one who has lost their keys.

Into the hall, "Mother? Mother?" he quipped louder each time.

He found her in the living room rocking in a chair. She sat proud holding court amongst four of his cousins. Cousin Jason sat tinkering at the piano. The piano cousin to the pool table, seldom used but always present. Jabber of the market and tinkering abruptly stopped when Benton entered the room.

From the royal chair, "Jonas, you remember your cousins don't you?"

He paid them no care, no respect, mites on a shade, boils on one's ass. In tandem they turned from him to her for response. The woman red like blood, rage and shame. Benton did not balk, care, or shiver.

Calmly, "Mother, why do you resent me so?"

The clock ticked away. The cousins, lost for words, only thought of defending the Queen. Stephen the eldest bore eyes of disgust at Benton and exited the room. Jason became nervous at the malevolence in Jonas's eyes. Thomas secretively begged Benton to have at her, to berate the old nasty bitch. The youngest, Lee, did not care for the drama, or its outcome, so fetched another Scotch.

" Jonas," his mother retorted.

"Just answer the question," he wildly demanded.

The remaining cousins lit like boys watching a bullfight.

"Boys would you leave us alone?" beckoned the old woman.

The door then shut leaving mother and son alone. The room, the house, the earth now quiet. Unknowing guests chatted in the other side of the house with no idea of the happenings in the room just beyond the spiral staircase. Knowing not to rock inheritance, the cousins meandered and reported nothing. Scotch drinking Lee wore a shit-eating grin. Jerry Benton entered the dining room to finish his cigar and Bourbon stupor. Mother and son went at it until the maid tapped on the door.

"We are sitting to dine Misses Benton," intoned the tremulous servant.

A silence, then whispering on the other side. The maid settled to knock again when Benton opened the door. Out came Mother escorted on his arm like the Imperial Family. He walked her to the dining room.

A hush as royalty entered. Abhorred, few rose for the Queen, for Alma, like Jerry, were exact opposites of Grandfather and the beloved, black sheepish Jon Jon. Mother stood at the head of the old maple table. She

46

thanked the group for their support, kindness and generosity. They smiled, the smile of one selling or buying a car.

The following days went as most in those types of days. The days then came to rest in the Mount Auburn Cemetery. The cousins brought Benton out to dine the night after Papa's burial and he had a surprisingly good time. He still felt the rush of having had at his parents.

The next morning, refusing the family limo, a green and white taxi drove him to the airport. As the cab passed the cemetery, Benton choked up, cried and smiled. When the cab passed the hospital near the river, his jaw began to ache. The taxi taxied on.

Arriving at the curb of Departures a sobbed overcame him as loneliness struck. Having seen it all before, the driver shut off the meter and let the passenger have his moment. This earned the man a lucrative tip.

The plane flew over cornfields and cows onto the heated tarp of California where Benton entered a commune of varying monk type personalities. Each morning he sat with the monks on the side of a mountain smoking something akin to heaven, so he thought. Eventually he sat alone. And eventually smoke was not enough.

In the mid 90s, he met Cheryl at a Narcotics Anonymous meeting. She sat there beat, grateful to be days clean, holding her young child's hand. She glanced across the room, the addicts, donuts and smoke, at the bearded smiling Benton, the eventual father to the bastard child and another.

4

HENRY FUR

Thirteen years of age, Henry Cass and his crew skulked what they named The Boulevard, Washington Street, Boston, Massachusetts, pizza enticing from every other corner. After lunch, the crew dispersed and Henry stood on the corner in expensive sneakers he stole from a kid at the Somerville Mall. Black skin with ruptures of acne, frizzy hair below its brim, a Steelers cap subliminally stated Henry's character defect. On that corner, at that moment, he came to a decision regarding Mother's soon to be birthday gift. The decision, soon to be antisocial act, would come to explain his future street name of Henry Fur.

The following Saturday arrived, Henry and the Steelers stood across the street from an establishment they cased a thousand times, so they would later explain to others with the same temperament. The Newbury Street window reflected to capture the bunch of thieves, the harsh January wind beckoning to penetrate their coats. Henry stuffed his cap into his oversized parka and crossed Newbury, his face hiding fear and teen pressure. He entered the couture place.

The crew remained, "Stay here and watch for the pigs."

An entrance chime chimed. A mid-aged white woman, sporting eighty-dollar dew, hesitantly went to the black boy.

"Can I help you?"

"Yeah, how much is the black fur coat in the window ova there?"

The woman smirked then smiled at the wannabe gangster.

"It is eighteen-hundred dollars, Sir. Plus taxes."

"Can I see it?"

Still hesitant, she said yes to the young black teen resembling the other guy on Miami Vice. What's his name? she thought.

As the woman unhinged the tiny lock securing the coat to the rack, Henry knocked her down, snatched Mom's mink and bolted out the door. A scream from inside the store, muffled by the gangster's antisocial pounding heart. As planned, the crew quickly walked in all directions with their matching parkas and black abyss hoods. Henry ran through the maze of cars at the corner of Arlington Street and crossed into the darkness of the Public Gardens.

In the shade of trees and quiet, he took off the parka and pulled a bag out of the pocket. He stuffed the mink into the bag and tossed the parka behind a bush onto a snoring homeless man. Now wearing red, Henry Cass was a Northeastern Husky. He walked sprightly but not so fast to be thought a thief. Reaching the nearby Commons, he slowed to a gait reflecting a student moving his stuff. The heart slowed, the mind eased. He felt a semblance of joy thinking of Momma's birthday, how it would lift her cancer stricken spirit for the while. How she would never ask where he got the mink. Apples never falling far from the trees. His radar ears twitched upon hearing the hyper-stepping of a sprinter. And smelled a pig.

Although joining the gang at twelve, a scam artist at nine, a suspected felon in the last minutes, Henry knew he was not tough. He recently appraised himself to be cowardly; a person who could never make it in the Charles Street Jail like Uncle Louis. He clung to the bag and bolted for dear life.

However, the cop had owned and honed a great skill, he ran at great speeds while adorning a slight beer gut. At the corner of Boylston and Tremont he reached out for, the Little Fuck, and could feel the frizz of the boy's afro. Henry could smell the pig breath, its vodka and mints, as the pair tumbled onto the wet, cold street. The boy tumbled as if a ball player quickly rolling onto his cleats. The cop slid in the slush as if to home plate, opening his arm with the city's latest droppings of roadway salt. They continued on.

Henry had a half block lead running like a Lasix riddled horse, running further and further from the Charles Street Jail, a spring in his step as if playing hoop at the Hurd Street Projects. Soon enough the pig was eight or nine lengths behind and closing. Henry made a left between Tuft's Medical Center and the Wang Theatre, when spared a speckle of luck. The loud beep of a horn is the last thing Officer Timothy Dolan remembered just prior to the taxi slamming his knee. As a large crowd surrounded the cop, Henry ran over the bridge above the burrow of rats to have cake with Momma. The heart still racing, he prayed to God for it not to implode.

Resentment

The following morning, while Henry slept, Dolan had surgery to repair a detached ligament that no longer held the knee in place. A plastic surgeon closed the deep facial cut obtained when Dolan was thrown onto broken glass. The injuries caused numbness, scarring, and an upcoming year of disability and the boredom of isolation. Post surgery Dolan lay in bed doped up, fucked up, wondering if the, "Fuckin' Nigger," lived near Columbus Ave?

Months later Officer Timothy Dolan was awarded a plague for bravery, an addiction to painkillers, and a festering hatred for the black race.

5

The making of a hooker

At the tender age of seventeen, Lisa (a.k.a. Lee, Liz, Angel, Bobbi) worked, breathed, and was the Zone for the last several years of her opiate fixated existence. It had not always been that very way of course. Not until she attended a horrific party in the 'Berry, the kind of party every church going father would not want his kin to attend. Lisa went anyway. The hours prior to the said party were Lisa Humboldt's last good moments on earth. Then it all changed. The sun no longer lit, the moon would guide her nights. It was the middle of summer, of ruthless 1989.

For some people luck seems to bring more of the same. When Martha Cass succumbed to Thoracic Cancer in her pristine bed at the Dana Farber, the unprotested Last Will, in clear type, stated her dying wishes. Hence, Henry Cass (a.k.a. Henry Fur) acquired the Deed to the old decrepit mansion sitting a block from Blue Hill Avenue on the Roxbury side of the Milton line. Henry took his luck as winning an adult version of Monopoly. A party was sure to follow. Henry had enrolled at Northeastern University for the upcoming fall semester in hopes of obtaining a business degree. However, he was already an entrepreneur of sorts, selling drugs and the sex of a younger female cousin.

The party began.

"Henry, this is my friend Lisa," announced Janine.

"Nice to meet your acquaintance," said the gangster/student as he attempted to shout above the volume of rap.

Instantaneously he was turned on by the girl's mulado skin. This was the very moment Lisa's problems began. Although high school girls attend many parties and return safe, it would not be true regarding Lisa. Not this ruthless night.

"Nice to meet you Henry. Is there anything to drink?" she inquired.

The question alone added to the girl's demise, for eventually alcohol spurns the effects of havoc. And eventually it will drone inhibitions.

High and giddy, just before midnight the girl relaxed in a Lazy Boy just as the rest of the guests partied on. Cheap cigar smoke caused her nostrils to twitch. Across the room, rolling another joint, Henry gazed at the mini-skirted mulado legs and decided he wanted her. Fuck the age thing he thought. Adding to Lisa's demise was her attraction to the punk who seemed to have it going on. She did not know of his dealings in drugs and flesh.

Most of the crowd dispersed around 2 AM onto other places of ill repute or sleep. Cousin Janine was in the filthy kitchen searching for mustard while the dogs sweated in the toaster oven. She did not know the condiment hid crustaceous behind the couch having been there since Super Bowl Sunday. Janine with her own plans for Roxbury College in fall, fell asleep on a kitchen chair while the tube steaks tanned like the Bentons in the Florida sun. Henry poked his head through the swinging kitchen door to spy his cousin. Finding her asleep, he knew it time to move in on the mulado in the Lazy Boy.

Lisa's head spun barleycorn wild, her face pushed into the stained leather spaceship. Her eyes opened to find a testosterone driven punk groping her breasts. She said nothing and smiled at Henry. The felonious male smiled back. Instead of gently kissing the young virgin, he demandingly grabbed her wrist and guided her hand to his crotch. A smile no longer placated his face, but a malevolent look expressing anger and entitlement. Although no longer smiling herself, Lisa shut her beautiful stoned eyes and convinced herself this must be love as marijuana and grain continued to distort her values and neurotransmitters. She struggled briefly against the punk then fell to a wave of submission.

"What the fuck are you doing?" Janine screamed, jealousy surfing her spine.

Upstairs in Mother's dead bed, a couple banged brass until startled by the loud scream. Exiting the ghost ridden room, they ski-sloped the creaky stairs to find Henry pummeling Janine's head against the wall. Jeremy tried to break up the malaise but his laughing fit only added to the chaos. Janine's head played tennis with the beer stained wall rattling Momma's old china. Now serious, Jeremy played good cop and held off Henry from committing another felony. Janine slid to the floor, stunned, confused, and somewhat euphoric from the rush of violence and drugs. A mouth full of blood, she smiled when spotting the mustard behind the Lazy Boy. Sensing the party duly over, Jeremy grabbed his lover and Janine, thanked his host, and headed for the old Dodge out front. Henry then rolled another joint, smiled at the mulado girl, and readied for round two.

The felon proceeded to rape the young girl. His forearm crushed down upon her mulado neck holding her in place. Lisa, young, naive, now trapped. Her head whirled in a storm of panic. When he forcefully entered her, the hymen ripped open her womanhood and blood surrounded his penis, oozing down her inner thigh and backside. The punk fucked away his crazed state of lust. Ingested chemicals made it impossible to ejaculate but he went at it anyway. The pounding act sobered Lisa a bit. Hollywood would have her detach at this point to the upper corner of the room, but she was aware of the wave of numbness as the huffing of the animal above stifled her inner prayers to Jesus. He rolled off her unsatisfied. As he slept, Lisa grabbed his hand and drifted to napping as distorted love lay next to her. The raped girl, no longer felt the need for prayer.

Entering and exiting a dozing nightmare, she awoke the next day around eleven o'clock no longer holding his hand. Henry lay on the sofa, his black penis maroon from crusted blood. A quiet house, a mansion back in the day, now a broken-down. A lost city. Devoid of guest and ghosts, a cool breeze descended from an upper floor window as the rapist lay dead to the world. The front door cracked open for the girl to leave at will. Evil still lurked.

Bruised neck, bloodied legs, ass and fingertips, coagulated crusty on the Lazy Boy. Lisa rose quietly from the vinyl-carnival-spaceship-ride. She stared at the man who took her virginity. Primarily, hate filled her mind and heart. She turned and walked into the kitchen to make breakfast.

As her bare mauve feet shuffled along the black tar skid marks of the old tile, she felt burning within her vagina. She store out the window, beyond Momma's knickknacks of small glass and pottery, into the open yard that was naked except an ancient Chevy and a rusted fridge. She thought of love. Henry. Life. She thought of an imagined child in her ripped womb and began to pray. A noise came from the other side of the scuffed lime-green door. She smiled thinking it was the father of her new baby. Her man.

The old saloon type door thudded open smashing the steel cabinet. She turned from the browning eggs to find a beast. It stood firm on its four legs and stared at her with a minimum of pupil in its glazier eyes. Lisa's eyes teared and lips quivered as the red Pit Bull strode toward her with its massive chest jutting side to side. Tears subsided as ice froze her mind. The shuffling noise of the beast getting closer. The deflowered girl stood a martyr waiting for an arrow as Henry continued snoring on the other side of the door.

Another door opened slamming the radiator at the far corner of the kitchen. Another dog ascended the darkness of cellar for its only noontime meal. This larger tan and white Pit Bull quickly inventoried the scene and became excited at the smell of blood. Insane with intrigue. Killer instinct inbred. Killer instinct taught. The latter in the last half decade. Overwhelmed with surreal horror, Lisa's legs gave out and she crumbled to the floor. Now Hollywood would have its glory as she finally dissociated and levitated to the corner ceiling of the room. As if sitting in a director's chair, she watched as the tan and white dog became maddened by the smell of blood and female. She watched the foam expand his pink and black tongue. The smaller red Pit Bull trotted out of the room. Lisa's heart pounded nearing implosion but her mind remained still as she watched the movie from the balcony seat. The larger dog carelessly sniffed and nibbled about her. She did not feel a thing as he mounted her.

The lime-green door opened again. A pervert, Henry watched the dog have its way. He did not stop it right off as he wanted Lisa to fear the dog and himself. She glanced at Henry with her dead face.

"Off King! Off!" he shouted.

He hit the dog's boney head with a broomstick as the animal did not care to stop. Whacking again at the spine, the dog finally backed off and went for its bone on the porch, pouting having liked the girl much better. The dog whimpered while chewing its bone. Blood dripped turning mulado skin to rust. This was Lisa's job interview for her soon to be occupation. Hearing the odd intervals of scratching noises, Henry peered up at the ceiling.

"Fuckin'rats!" he screamed.

Months later the bank took the house and the pair never made it to college. Soon enough they shared an apartment on LaGrange Street in the Combat Zone. Lisa admiringly stared at her man, flutters in her chest, and while Henry slept, she reached for the syringe dangling from his arm and used it herself. And warmness overcame her. Her man wakened. She thanked him for being a good provider as blood dripped from her arm to wet kiss the dirty floor. Bed bugs bit her legs. From his own stoned state, Henry peered up at Lisa and nodded as if approval to something. She placed the paraphernalia in the old night table renting to roaches. While nodding, she attempted to straddle him. Henry now asleep, she rolled off.

Dilated eyes, she confessed to one of her gods, "I love you."

King panted in the corner and the walls began to scratch.

Freddie

Freddie Nolan thought he would crack on his twenty-ninth day of sobriety. Kneeling at the side of an old rickety bed, he prayed to the same Higher Power that helped him maintain abstinence from barleycorn a decade back. Or so was his belief.

Three young men, white shirts, black ties, were simply doing as taught back in Utah, what Elders stated to be rightful, what Moroni expected of them. It did not matter much they were in the Combat Zone, for Moroni and their books would protect them. The two younger headed for the Hyundai parked around the corner. However, the oldest was sap from a tree seeping faith and tried harder to believe. Lester entered the Y.M.C.A. on Boylston to further hone his skills in Moroni sales.

Security guard Bobby descended to the basement to investigate rattraps. Unbeknown to all, he was getting head from a single mother who craved male attention. Lester duly marched by the unoccupied security desk leaving the guestbook untouched on the yellow tarnished table. Ignorant of the road ahead, chagrin wore brightly on the youth's acne as Lester pushed the top button within the square copper panel and waited for the elevator.

The door opened with a loud slam inviting Moroni's soldier into the outdated ride. Without thought, he pressed number five wondering if Satan might live there. He thought of the obstacles Joseph Smith, founder of his religion, endured back in the day. With fantastical thinking, Lester imagined the button panel another tablet for Smith to transcribe. The steel cage abruptly halted two inches from the fifth floor. The door opened, banged and rattled. Lester marched on. One gleeful smile. The look of high in his eyes.

"Right or left?" he asked his god.

Tripping on the floor's lip, he stumbled into the wall. He bent over to retrieve his fumbled books and bibles and inhaled a century of urine and nicotine remnants.

A voice mumbled from beyond the dark egg white wall, "Get the fuck outta..." It faded just as fast.

Eyebrows raised, pupils adjusting to the pallets of dark and dark, the youth peered to his left. A window open, a small space, a brick wall just beyond. Soiled diapers, bloodied syringes and tampons wafted up the small space from the four floors below. Lester entered the hall to the right. In the dark, a fire extinguisher jutted out and tapped the boy's arm. He hopped sideways.

"Damn," he cursed then prayed to Moroni again.

He fell to his knees and pleaded, "Dear God, please pardon my impatience in this moment of recent discomfort. I am stricken with my own weaknesses of shame. Please forgive me."

Lester fetched his books again and walked the humid hall this Saturday afternoon. Freddie Nolan spied through the slit door of 5K. How the fuck did he get in here? He shut the door and went back to self-absorption to forget what his diabetic eyes may have seen.

Bibles, books and prayers, Lester walked the hall, skin soaked with humidity and fear. He rapped softly at the first door he came upon.

The softest of whisper, "I will make you repent," he warned to the supposed Satan on the other side of the door, and did not rap again.

Meanwhile, Freddie was on his knees in 5K begging God to stand between him and a drink, "Relieve this obsession Heavenly Father."

Freddie craved cheap wine more than the world he was born into. He thought of younger days when he made money on his knees instead of prayer. Recalling the rapists, thieves of the flesh, diseases that crawled his skin, back in the day, his fake teeth grinded. Between his chin and bed lay the Big Book of Alcoholics Anonymous. Freddie and Lester had commonalities. Each prayed to a savior. Each lacked faith. Each still believed.

5K. Tap, tap. Freddie rose from the side of the bed then Lester and he stood on opposite sides of the door. They pressed their faces to the old varnish, its cracks like the face of an old whore. Respective bibles in hand, forgetful due to self-absorption, Freddie hoped it was not his sponsor picking him up to go retrieve day old donuts for the meeting near the State House.

The whore's old face said, Tap, tap.

"Who is it?" inquired whispering Freddie.

Nothing. Tap, tap.

"Who is it?" he said louder.

"My name is Lester Williams, Sir."

Relieved it not his sponsor, Freddie opened the door expecting security's warning of Eddie Arnold being too loud for other patrons the night before.

Instead, he opened the door to witness a pamphlet coming toward his diabetic eyes. Cartoon characters depicted Jesus and children as if a coloring book. Then Freddie's eyes adjusted to the darkness.

Spontaneously, the old man screamed, "Nigger," and swung a decrepit fist at the youth.

Lester moved backward then watched the old fool follow the decrepit fist to the floor with a thump.

"Jesus H. Christ," Freddie roared from the stained rug where roaches traveled in darkness to another buffet and rent controlled housing.

Down the hall a door opened with the arthritic turn of brittle metacarpals, a very long time since the hand serviced a john. And Freddie continued to curse.

"What's going on here?" the old hooker's voice inflecting raspy decades of vodka and smokes.

"Go back in Millie, it's another salesman for the Lord."

She retreated to her cubicle carrying dialogue amongst herself.

Freddie peered up from the floor, "Who do you think you are thinking you know the Lord, you self righteous nigger?"

Belittled, Lester hoped the old man would swing again as he always loathed being called, characterized, or becoming nigger.

And Freddie again, "You think you know where souls are headed, do ya? You put on your god armor and go out into the world to do good, and mean to, but come up short. That is why he came. You try to sell your cult to the desperate. Good luck to you Columbus. Look around son. Tell me, can you ever, really believe in God, Son, any Holy Ghost, or whatever you're pushing?"

Freddie stood from the carpet like a boxer in his last fight. Mildred Zimmer suddenly appeared in the hallway and the youth froze. His pants became warm and wet when the leathered hag pulled something shiny from her smock pocket. Finding no need for prayer, Lester bolted for the backstairs craving the necessity of sunlight.

"And you, you piece of alcoholic shit, get your ass to that stupid little meeting or I'll kick your ass too! You hear?"

He nodded then barricaded himself behind the reef thin door. When the hall was clear, Mildred lifted the metal to her face. She opened it and smiled her horse teeth at the mirror inside. A malevolent cackle expressed gratitude for the few moments of stimulation.

9

Brothers Peter and Mickey, 1988

Three things crave a good blast of arctic snow, men who own snowplows, weathermen, and kids listening to WBZ Radio for school cancellations. Here enter the brothers Peter and Mickey, camped in front of the television one white day until the wanted news arrived... "Winchester, Winthrop, Woburn." Revelry.

"You boys be good," ordered the devote mother setting off to serve coffee and the like to city workers and the like, black beauties in her body and smock to survive the elements of snow and lethargy.

Mickey doodled in a notebook while Chuck Barris drooled on *The Gong Show*. Older brother Peter rose from the patched sofa.

"I'm goin' back to bed. Do not! I repeat, do not wake me."

Mickey bobbed his head acknowledging Peter's command. He returned to doodling while Gene Gene the Dancing Machine shimmied on.

Peter, the tall lanky troglodyte of Woburn High School, proceeded to get stoned as Led Zeppelin peered from the bedroom wall. Soft cushions surrounded his ears and Queen rocked at the eighth level of volume, bass 6, treble 9. When Freddie Mercury hit the first high note, so was Peter high. Fingers and thumb scanned beneath the bed, a spider for food, emerging from the linty rug with porn. Pondering the skin models within, he pumped away and ejaculated onto a Kiss t-shirt. He threw the shirt and magazine to the floor, rolled on his side, and fell asleep at the feet of Jimmy Hendricks. The magazine lay wrinkled and stained on the unkempt rug. Lint balls rolled like tumbleweed over the *Playgirl* magazine.

The notebook long tossed and shrapnel of cereal painfully stuck to the roof of Mickey's palate. *All My Children* introduced on the old black and white. The brothers slept into the latter half of afternoon. They woke near tandem around five. The seven clocks in the six rooms said so. Mickey scanned the freezer while Peter coughed into the concert air of his bedroom.

"Pete," yelled the brother. Then again.

"What?"

"Want somethin' to eat?"

What you makin'? asked the concertgoer.

"Waffles," replied the eighth grader.

"Yeah," Peter screamed above The Who.

Winter's short sun managed little to melt the six inches bestowed and stowed upon Woburn and its industrial affect. Mother called from the donut shop to see if the boys were okay. Of course, they were. Following waffles, Mickey watched The Pink Panther on the snowy screen as his brother got stoned at another AC/DC concert.

The old phone rang.

"I'll be home in an hour. What do you boys want from McDonald's?"

"Pete," Mickey yelled. "Pete!"

"What?" screamed from the concert hall.

"Ma's on the phone. What d'ya want from McDonald's?"

"What I always fuckin' get."

"Pete wants..."

"When you hang up this phone tell your brother to watch his mouth or I'll wash it out with soap," Ma spouted, the beauties wearing down.

"I know what you want. I just wanted to let ya know I'll be home soon. I love you. Bye."

"I love you too Ma," the last words Gladys ever heard from her son.

10

Night of the Rat revisited, 1999

Peter

Massachusetts can be brutal in winter especially if you are a promiscuous homosexual headed out to meet another online date in the midst of the woods along the Fellsway. Yet, the bone cracking wind, wet shoes, and stalling Ford Escort did not impede Peter's craving for cock. The two agreed to meet along a gray stretch of highway in nearby Stoneham where the exodus of leaves left the forest bare heightening the chance of getting caught with one's pants down. And always the threat of the dreaded basher. Fear aside, like a child discarding God after Mother's premature death, Peter set out to meet Dan from Scituate, salivating and erect. Anticipating gay reality porn, he hungered on.

The Stoneham side of Route 93 is beautiful in early winter. Landscape appeared as if a Christmas card. Snow held off the last few days, started to melt, then froze in the evening hours. Squirrels hid in burrows along the frozen pond like their distant cousin Rat. Fury heads slept next to nuts like patients at the local psyche ward. Peter parked the car and was much relieved to spot only one other auto in the dirt lot. He exited the heated shitbox and descended the footpath darkening at the supper hour. Icicles hung from naked trees. One hit his shoulder in the darkness like the basher months ago in the Ratskeller Club. He hopped sideways and huffed. Blood seemingly left his ungloved hands to flood the veins in his manhood. His erection led him like a compass to Dan in the woods.

Between boulders, bushes and trees stood Dan in a Navy Pea Coat. Arctic cold freezing tears on branches, the two men nervously smiled as each prayed not to be bashed. They only relaxed when holding the other man's penis. As Peter, "Stephan from Somerville," leaned against a large boulder, Dan dropped to the earth and felt the warmth now in his mouth. The wind crackled and snapped the black thicket of trees heightening their sense of adventure. After a short while, he told Dan to stop so he could return the favor. Dan lay on the cold earth. Peter then felt the heat of dick as he bobbed on it. He stopped, crawled up and whispered into Dan's ear. The pair stood then Peter leaned over a fallen tree. Dan spat in his hand, rubbed the spit onto his oversized cock, and jammed it into the waiting ass. Its girth caused the bottom to grunt. Peter grabbed, his by then flaccid cock, and pulled at it as if finding its pleasure for the first time. Dan informed he was close. The bottom made sure to jack himself quick and hard. Friction and force, like trees, ice, sky and moon, the magnificence of nature had its way and the two squelched harmonious. As the Boston workforce jockeyed along 93 North, so did Peters cum turn tapioca on a bed of pine needles. And the lovers laughed

"Did you hear those squirrels rustling?" said the older top.

"I don't think those were squirrels Dan," said the sore ass bottom.

And the lovers laughed again. The highway bright over there.

Spent Peter entered the home he was embarrassed to inhabit at his current age, on account Uncle Theo took over the mortgage. And, "It sucks," to share a bathroom with a brother and his live-in, skanky girlfriend. Yet, the three somehow got along.

"Pete?" echoed from the cellar where photo remnants of Ma and Christmas remained.

"Yeah, it's me. Where's the lovely wife to be?"

"Don't know."

"I'm leaving in half an hour, be ready or I'm leavin' without ya. I'm going to take a shower. What are you doin' down there?"

"Looking for photos of Ma. "

While Peter showered, Mickey ascended from the moldy asbestos cellar and dashed madly so not to miss his ride. Twenty-eight minutes later, Mickey joined his brother entering the shitbox Cinderella, a notebook in hand like a guarded child. Tonight Peter wore a red mini dress. The younger thought nothing of this having seen it all before.

Cinderella vibrated the now Tourette like twins down 93 South. Autos swerved clear of its blackened emissions, large knuckles and painted face. Mickey's eyes pasted to an open notebook, he then looked at his older brother seat dancing to Natalie Cole and thought, What the fuck?

Peter's mind journeyed beyond the lights and scattering cars, to a world where people visit now and then. A world of reminisce, some go there more often; a place where one can think of past scenarios either lived or dreamed. Scenarios twisted with a speck of denial. And this is not necessarily bad unless one's life is enraptured in such a state, driving a shit box, a set of large knuckles turning the tremulous wheel, the others adjusting the pseudo-silk mini riding up shaven legs headed for the Combat Zone. And so, Cinderella proceeded to jockey as if making the last turn at Suffolk Downs, bright lipstick showboating the smiling face of a sex addict being sucked off in the woods. Sex thoughts riddled Peter's mind, stimulating him as Mickey rode shotgun. Passing the Somerville Projects, precum saturated the dress with crimson spots about the groin. Pollock meets Mapplethorpe. Just another form of artistic freedom. Loneliness, that sad state of affairs, crushed for the moment while thinking of Dan in the woods. The memory ran Peter's mind like a gay flick clicking from the projector in Room 2 of the Art Cinema on Tremont. Teared eyeliner as Cole belted out the last song on the decayed cassette player. Clown face Peter, euphoric, going to meet her one true love.

Bald tires slightly skidding in the slush as Cinderella sled onto Stuart Street. A right and a right, she handed a ten to the man in the tin booth and parked the car in the lot next to Dominic's Restaurant & Pub.

"I'll be back between twelve-thirty and one," warned she to her sibling. "If you're not here, you had better pray you make the last train at North Station."

"I'll be here."

Peter walked away. Mickey stood in the crowded lot.

"Well?" he inquired aloud.

"Well what?" Peter hollered back.

"You goin' to wish me luck?"

"For what?"

"My act asshole."

"You don't need luck. You're my brother."

7:43 PM, while cars beeped at the, "Fuckin' freak," in the crosswalk, Mickey turned and gazed at the neon sign where he hoped to get his big break, Nick's Comedy Stop.

11

Jessenia

Jessenia now walked along Washington Street in her red mini flaunting her manly and womanly wares. Almost simultaneous with the clicking of her heals, a familiar Town Car pulled to the curb.

"Hi Jessenia," the old man said, his turkey neck flapping side to side.

"Hey Baby," the pre-op replied.

Moments gone, her red dress and ass were warming on the heated leather seat.

Right on Essex, right on Harrison, left at Kneeland, right on Hudson.

"Pull over after that fire hydrant. And kill the heat," she commanded.

Six minutes later, fifty dollars gone, the old man sighed victorious as liquid managed its way out of the ancient urethra, smeared lips pumping it into a state funded condom.

The retired State Rep dropped his date at the corner of Stuart near the dental school. Jessenia perused in tooth pick heels and acquired another four dates within the hour. Money abundant, she stashed it in her brassiere as if an ATM to deposit and withdraw at will. At the end of her eleventh date the Zone was cold and dead like squab under Mr. Po's knife at a local restaurant. The arctic air and meds made Jessenia's testicles cashews as if in a dish at the same place. She waited and waited along Tremont Street.

LaGrange Street approximates 200 yards running parallel between Boylston and Stuart. The Glass Slipper strip joint is established on the dark street. Other buildings have dark entrances no one seemingly enters or exits. Seemingly. If one were inside such a place, they were beyond praying to Saint Anthony for lost things. Morning was night and night was day. Jessenia walked down the said street. Nearing the Slipper, she took a left onto

Tamworth and headed for the corner at the Y.M.C.A. An auto sitting alone like an abandoned child, she stopped and bent to a car mirror. The moonlight reflected just enough for Jessenia to apply her last face of the evening. Then she was smiling. Feeling the urge for weed, she removed a joint and lighter from her handbag. For privacy, she stepped into the alley of Lowell Court, a grotto of rats and darkness, and proceeded to get high. When hearing a noise near the dumpster, Jessenia dropped the paraphernalia and quickly exited the alley. She trotted, then sauntered for the relief of a well-lit place, jittery from a nervous system that craved drugs of one type or another. With no chemical drugs on her person, she relied on her old standby once again and decided to slut out to the flesh. And with this decision she walked some more.

She clacked her tall red spikes on the frozen pavement at the corner of Beech Street and peered down to Chinatown. It was 12:11 a.m. She frowned because her true love T had not shown. She waited a short while then the prompting of addiction nudged her to walk on.

She crossed the street to LaGrange, men in autos cheering him/her on. Out of the Glass Slipper stumbled two sailors wearing blue and white. Heavy Pea Coats and bourbon warmed them. Jessenia craved her coat back at the car. The pair of sailors spotted her. The taller enlisted man bent to his comrade's ear. Jessenia got a hit of sex-smack merely knowing the act to follow, an act she would truly perform for free.

She sang aloud Joe Walsh's, "Life's been good to me so farrrrr…"

"Hey sweetness," said the shorter sailor to the red dress.

They swaggered toward her.

"What is it fellas?"

"You a cop?" said Short.

"I'm too sweet and pretty to be a cop. But I can't say I'm not a pig."

They trio laughed

"You wanna make some money, honey?" inquired Tall.

"I love poets. What else you got?" said Jessenia's street witted sarcasm.

Three faces wore three smiles on three desperate faces. Erections hid behind cloth for the while.

Eyes dotted the black buildings, having seen it all before. Ever so quiet a curtain moved from one of the dark glass cubicles. A scarred hand connected to a scarred arm connected to a scarred spirit. Having hustled her wares earlier in the night, the woman behind the curtain was high on some, "Really good stuff." Her apnea pimp lay sleeping in a bed barely wide enough for his large ass. Seeing her reflection in the dingy window, the woman became repulsed at the face turning older with each injection of smack. She looked over her boney shoulder at her lover and boss.

Tall, Short, and Jessenia walked past the flickering neon of the Slipper, the streets only illumination save the moon. They turned onto Tamworth and walked the sloping hill of pavement, its slush and ice. Her fear of former alley sounds stifled by the urge to temporarily treat a sex addiction, she led them into the alley at Lowell Court.

"I like it in the ass if you don't mind?" she inquired and request.

High on alcohol and sex the three men laughed. Tall and Small leaned their backs against the wall with the slightest push of Jessenia's French nails. Giggles. Rats quietly walked along the adjacent wall to scoot unnoticed up the street. In the last of alley light, the sailors grinned and unzipped themselves. Jessenia dropped to her knees and silently prayed to different saints that the sailors would not want to touch her privates. Small was first. A brief period of friction, the reek of burnt rubber, he came in her condom mouth. He winked at his taller comrade, the same wink shared when they fucked a minor in Jakarta. Short moved deeper into the alley and lit a smoke. Just beyond him stood a door to nowhere at the alley's end.

Tall grabbed Jessenia by the chin, guided her upward, leaned her into the wall, and grabbed the hips of what he perceived a hot filly. She winced as the unprotected flesh entered her ass. Tall fucked away while recalling scenes watched in an old German cinema, its screen still cracked from the Cold War. Then he was done. Jessenia cringed at the stench of bleach smelling cum now on the ground. Olfactory recall of abuse, she smiled anyway and stuck the eighty dollars in her A.T.M. The sailors thanked "Roberta" at the mouth of the alley. They quickly walked away, as did she.

Up in the gray window the voyeuristic junkie watched the show. She remained dry, for a babysitter knocked the fun out of sex when she was nine. She hid behind the musty veil of curtain as blue lights flashed the brick and concrete walls along the street.

12

Mickey

Trodden plush stairs, the welcoming mat to many desperate comedians. Mickey descended them quickly for his act did not go as planned. An unlaced shoelace tripped him up but he recovered with equilibrium of a former high school hockey star. He thanked Bobby the doorman for getting him on the list to perform that amateur night. The perfectly groomed Mafioso wannabe nodded while sipping coffee diluted with brandy, or vice versa. Perfect Vitalis hair shined in the strategically lit lobby of Nick's. Bobby thought nothing of Mickey's acrobats having seen it all before. As the distraught comedian reached for the exiting door a head popped out from the swinging doors that separated the lobby from the main room of the comedy club.

"Good show Mick," congratulated another amateur act.

"Thanks man," and the distraught went into the cold wet kiss of night.

He tucked his chin toward the clavicle to diminish the sleet storm pummeling his face. Wind howled down J shaped Warrenton Street making sounds of a flute. Wet sweated and dripped on the neon sign of Nick's. It read, *This Week Chris Zito George McDonald Eddie Brill D.J. Hazard Hosted by Tony V. & Billy Martin.* Nearing the midnight hour, Mickey's face numbed as he crossed the lot where Cinderella stood shivering. Distorted cognitions mingled with grandiose delusions to invade the comic's mind. He recalled the show, the lack of applause, the bereft stare of the couple in the front row. These thoughts crossed the synapses like the rat shit floating along the curb to the sewers below the city. Mickey's misfortune, Richie the manager of Nick's could smell the rat shit too. As the comic exited the stage, the crowd turned insane with cheering, jeering, and a deafening applause for the unique act. Yet, Mickey did not hear it. He only noticed the bereft couple in the first row.

And he did not know they had been fighting before the show. Low self-esteem, self-respect, self-absorption, and self-devaluation, exuded lack of confidence on the comic's face. The crowd saw him sweat then smelled the feces of rat. Richie smelled it too. And the manager knew rat shit was not good for any business venture.

Mickey tried to open Cinderella's door and it was locked. A sense of stress came about him like impending doom, as when Ma died in the, "Stupid fuckin' hospital." Standing on this frozen lot, five months clean, Mickey decided to pick up drugs. Like that. Just fuckin' do it, he thought. He made the call from a flu ridden public phone at the corner to see the guy on Comm. Ave. a fellow comic recommended. A half hour later, he walked out of the apartment. Mushrooms in belly, tablets in pocket, he headed back for Cinderella to catch his ride.

He passed Nick's again. This time the red and white sign vibrated and spoke as he peered up from the littered sidewalk.

"Don't worry your name will be here too," it said.

Happy and content, not feeling his cold sneaker feet, he popped a tab of acid and swallowed it with spit. Fuck, he thought, it's only a little past midnight.

Unbeknown to the user, the acid was concocted and produced down south by a chemist who was two years short of a Master's degree. The chemist was good at his trade. But, one day feeling rushed and high himself, he produced a batch from leftovers that were to travel that night via an obese woman and her two bastards bound by government surplus cheese. And the airport guards did not search her for they did not feel the need to touch the woman's fat. Shortly after swallowing the bad hit of southern hospitality, Mickey took a trip of his own.

He stood on the corner of Washington and Stuart staring over at Sonny's, the best fuckin' pizza joint. The famed establishment melted as the acid hit harder than the current air killing rats. He leaned and pressed his hot face against a utility pole with etchings of Ozzy, Marty, 1982, 99. Pupils crazily dancing worms to a flashlight. The mind a defenseless flounder against a fisherman's bat, Mickey was higher than the recent state taxes. He shut, then opened his eyes to a drugged world that appeared like a fucked up dream.

It finally happened, Apocalypse hit; end of reality at the hand and gumption of God. Aids and Apartheid now trivial. Rent could be late. People lay and sat on the ground as Mickey peered up Washington Street. Lights out at the all-night porn theater? Unheard of. Zombie-likes poured out of the Intermission Lounge and Naked I to lie in the street. Tina the Whore stood in front of the bookstore with a number burnt in her forehead. A branded crucifix inches away on her cheek. A chain and medallion hung from her neck and she kissed it often and prayed. Only few others mirrored Tina's marks of salvation. A priest sat near her uncontrollably sobbing, remembering all the children he destroyed with his insatiable libido and perverted manipulations. Mickey's tripping mind floated up to Jordan Marsh where people's lives passed before them. Most screamed in panic. A woman gently placed her baby on a wooden bench and kissed its soft branded head. Gratitude swamped her. Numberless herself, she lay on the street to be trampled by a police horse, cop, and chariot. Sirens blaring. Then all the people of this place became aware of the promised day. It hit fast, not symbolic like many had thought. Abrupt in its conquer, cries became shrieks and only the branded remained standing. They prayed for their loved ones and foes all of which remained without mark. Some of the standing appeared Pollyannaish. Others simply content. These branded few, and the babies, and the nomads of the alley, all standing, all saved. The numberless could not and did not pray. In this dismal hour of chaos God refused to hear it.

Guilt infiltrated Mickey's mind as he judge himself sinful, sacrilegious with these thoughts and dreams. The acid did not care. Skies darkened from reddening clouds. The sun briefly appeared like a broken yoke and dripped sizzling onto melting buildings. Trumpets blared, sirens whirred, alarms alarmed. People of the Zone watched their world become smaller and useless. Down to size. They saw the futility in its degenerative blocks. A puzzle piece of shame. Mickey's mind floated back to the corner at the pole. And this is where he met the Lord.

As prophesized, Jesus on horse. The horse white. Then purple. Then black. Then it... all the people stood now on the curbs, alleys and streets to salute their General. The General serene, stared solely at Mickey Nolan. The pristine white horse floated inches above the icy pavement and the addict felt euphoric as the Lord approached him.

'Do you want salvation my son?" Jesus asked.

The Lord wore the smock of a retired mother. Its radiant colors enmeshed and swirled. The horse now flat black, a shade the addict Mickey painted model cars in his youth. Jesus smiled. Smoke exuded from his toothless mouth. Mickey emoted fear and remained tentative in trusting the Lord. And he never answered the Lord's question.

Then all the questions he had asked God over the years appeared on the marquee of the Pilgrim Theatre. Tina the Whore approached the man/god and offered her services. Jesus nodded. Mickey stood baffled and titillated when she went onto her hands and knees below the stallion. The multitudes watched as if it were Vaudeville at the Old Howard in Scollay Square. Back in the day. Tears fried the faces of the crowd as Tina serviced the horse. The horse then whinnied. She rose from beneath the satisfied animal with her numbered forehead. Jesus helped her up onto the horse with his boney bloodied hand. The crowd roared having noticed her numbered forehead changed to 666.

"This woman has saved you. Look upon her as if my own child, my own seed. Be kind and honorable to her for she is your light. And nomads of the alley feel fortunate, I have given you salvation for you came to me as children," the Lord spoketh and said.

The multitude became frenzied as the whore reached in her bag and produced a sickle knife. They roared like lions as she grabbed the Lord's unfashionable hair and decapitated Him. The head bounced on the icy street, a rubber ball for the crowd to kick. Jesus' bloody torso got off the spent horse and walked amongst the crowd. The roaring stopped. His bloody hand numbered their foreheads and caused them to fall to the earth, to shake like eels. Eels turned to snakes. Hellish shrieks stifled to a hellish humming drone.

"This woman's faith has saved the lot of you," announced the rolling head now across the street.

The horse trotted slowly to Mickey and laid his velvety soft neck to his face. A wave of love overcame the addict. The satanic whore descended her beast. She knelt and took Mickey in her mouth. As he floated in those moments of pre-orgasmic delight, the whore jerked and severed the penis with her razor-like teeth. Blood sprayed the Whore's face, the horse, the ground, the sky. Mickey collapsed and felt only the pain of sorrow flooding his Catholic mindset. The Mass Water Resource Authority cemented earth opened. Its pit swallowed the Whore and her equestrian john. The multitude of snakes hissed. Mickey returned from his high. Back in reality, he crumbled to the earth with a thud. Occasional strolling pedestrians and pederasts walked around the fallen man. And Mickey Nolan overdosed and died, while their Christianity napped.

13

Officer Timothy Dolan

Black Irish cop, black hair, snow white face, green eyes the spectacular colors of stained glass aligning the ceiling of Saint Mary's in hometown Charlestown, Timmy Dolan walked Precinct One the Irish version of Adonis.

Months prior at the punk age of nineteen, Dolan became a Boston cop unlike the roofing relatives and lineage of boat makers before him. And he previously contemplated the trades. Fuck that, he thought just before forking over two grand to ace the cop test. Another ten to get on the department.

Months after sworn in by the mayor, coworkers were baffled why the best-looking man on the force was not taken or at least spoken for. More baffling to the gals in the department was how he would flirt and never asked them out. And this caused resentment. And the whispering commenced. And some of these resentful women, with their anger and envy, thought of Mickey at night while they fucked their husbands or boyfriends, or both. They had no idea the abuse Dolan sustained between the ages of seven and twelve at the hands of Aunt Debbie, the devious pedophilic babysitter. Timothy, Timmy, Tim, T, Peanut, tried to bury the pain of shame. And he thought he had done a good job of it. However, a dark side boiled and eventually submerged from the onetime altar boy. Subsequently, compulsorily, he liked sex way too much. And privately behind the blue suit and badge, he thought himself a newt.

A spotlight flickered the red and black walls of LaGrange Street making streaks of orange, blue and gray. Just before 1 AM., Dolan searched for deviant behavior when he noticed two sailors staggering near the corner of Tamworth. The squad car let out a foghorn roar causing curtains to move in black cubicles on buildings. Half way up Tamworth's slope, a red mini dress stopped in her high-heeled tracks. Dolan peered beyond the blue and whites and noticed Jessenia. The sailors frowned as the car inched its way toward them.

"Go on your way," he said to the drunken men.

They did not argue and staggered toward Washington Street and headed for the Charlestown Navy Yard. Patrons exiting the Naked I cheered when Small violently vomited vodka and pickled eggs onto a newspaper machine. And some of the people of the Zone headed home for the night.

Back on LaGrange, Dolan and Jessenia became hard having known each other prior.

"How you doin' Baby?" she asked, blowing menthol cancer into the rat killing chill.

"Hop in."

Dolan drove up LaGrange toward Tremont and parked the car in the darkness of the alley like street. Jessenia wasted no time and took the cop in her mouth. While his cop boots pressed against the government shagged floor, and his cop knees buckled in a heightened state of arousal, and her mini rode high, and her ass warmed, neither cared about disease. And the cop's body jerked on the coldest night of 1999.

"Thanks Baby," they said in tandem.

Jessenia opened the door and walked into the unforgiving night, happy, happy, having seen her man T.

14

Mr. and Mrs. Fur

A decade after moving in, "For only a couple months," the common law cubicle of the Furs sat kitty-corner to the Glass Slipper on the second floor of a rat-infested place. The Furs remained for the rent was cheap enough to keep the track marks fresh. Lisa's used up appearance made it difficult to sell her wares so she sold at liquidation prices. The Zone's promissory ten-year stamp seeped into the one time immaculate girl.

On the coldest of nights, after another melee over white powder not used to bake, Liza stared at her reflection in the dirty bedroom/kitchen window. Two hours into withdrawal, the desperate woman reflected on her past and present. The future had no thought. She turned and stared at her lover. Invasive thoughts invaded. Promptings nudged to kill. Henry lay snoring as if he had never woke from the morning of her whore induction.

"The unfairness of it all," she said to no particular deity.

Cognitions of jamming a dirty syringe into his chest flooded her psyche. She remembered having similar thoughts just prior to King ending in a puddle of blood. And the memory of the beating, and the crack of the bat, and the trip to Boston City Hospital, for killing, "the fuckin' dawg." Therefore, to survive the current state of madness, she thought of Momma and Christmas like the social worker suggested.

This worked for a while then Lisa's jonesin' withdrawal catapulted the whore back from the land of fairies and snowflakes. She again looked out the window at the gray city, the moon reflecting her droopy dog eyes. At the limits of peripheral site, she noticed two men exiting the alley of Lowell Court. Then the red dress. The rats bouncing along the gutter toward Boylston. Fuckin' rats, she thought. Lisa turned and walked toward the door as if to leave.

"Without thought, planning, or pretense," the Assistant D.A. would later claim, "the defendant grabbed the bat, swung it, and struck Henry in the head causing the injuries that killed him."

Lisa would testify, "I had enough of his shit," thus sealing the sentence of manslaughter.

"He wasn't a man," she shouted to the jury. "Henry Fur was a fuckin' prick."

And Henry slept for good.

15

Freddie Nolan

Moroni departed a decade prior. Ray Arnold continued singing from the small speakers in the corner of the ancient room, the room a witness to lost souls over the years. A musty room where a handful were said to have died. Slightly after 2 AM, Freddie drifted off listening to the Country Opera. The Big Book of A.A. in hand, a smoke fell from the other as he oozed into dream.

Little Frederick walked toward his deceased mother in the government issued home of childhood. Father upstairs with sister Kate, Corporal Nolan's fatigues lay folded pristine and orderly at the foot of the bed. Mother and son Frederick could not look at each other as they heard the rhythmic noise pounding louder than Ray Arnold on the living room radio. Mother decided to play a game with her embarrassed son. So they did. They sat on the sofa in the dank room of the parlor. The buxom-blonde lit a cigarette, held it between rust stained fingertips and sang, "Green, green, grass of home." Little Frederick so, so happy watching Mother doing Vaudeville. Until the atmosphere changed.

The pounding stopped. All quiet in the house. The family dog remained buried in the back corner of the yard. Ray Arnold stuttered, "Garr, Grrrr, Grrrreeeen." Little Frederick thought of Porky Pig and let out an uncomfortable giggle. Mother placed her cigarette on the arm of the sofa, turned and smiled at her only child's crystal blue eyes. In a fleeting moment of fucked up decision, she placed her jagged nails on his crotch. Her green eyes now dark as black pupils overran the entirety of the eye, then the socket, then the face, and so on. Little Freddie's mind snapped within the dream, snapped into a state given many diagnosis later in the boy's life. Numbness overcame him. Confusion of the confusing of the dream turned nightmare. He could not understand why his pee pee got hard. The slut, the whore, the mother trembled in fear and excitement as she craved and destroyed a younger version of her husband. And Little Freddie could no longer look at his mother.

"Look at me handsome," she commanded.

He peered further and further away counting the patterns within the Oriental rug.

"Look at your mother," she shouted, rubbing him harder.

Finally, he turned to her with shameful eyes that would never see another day of esteem. The darkness of her face overcame her body and darkened the room. She opened her parched mouth, stench expelling, cigarette teeth bending toward its prey. Mother's satanic eyes winced as the boy went soft beneath the friction of OshKosh. Her angelic beauty could not be seen.

"What's wrong little boy, did I scare you?"

His spine chilled and his head hurt as if hit with a balpene hammer. The satanic female rose from the orange vinyl sofa and floated toward the opening sky. The sun hit her face and she rocketed back to the floor.

"What's wrong little boy, did I scare you?" she repeated.

Freddie's mind on fire as Mother lay there in white. The fire raged within the boys head, and then he awoke.

The arm of the chair smoldering, about to set ablaze from the fallen butt, he dropped the Big Book and retrieved the pot of coffee sitting on the sill and extinguished the doom of dream.

"Fuck you," he cursed to the moldy room for suddenly craving drink after all these years.

He placed the old pot on the old sill, placed his old palms down on the old cracked paint, peered out the old window with old diabetic eyes. His old ears heard a muffled moan and the shuffling of feet. Commotion. The noise reminded him of Vivaldi for no apparent reason. Freddie opened the old window, squinted his eyes and focused. Down and across in the alley, a pair of legs stuck out from behind the dumpster like the Wicked Witch. Another person ran from the alley, darted across the street and hid in the alcove of an abandoned business front. Asking God for help to do his Heavenly Father's will, ol' Freddie picked up the old phone on the old side table and dialed 911. He reported what he had seen, and pranced for the old door.

16

Benton

Early fall, '97, metered mail found its way to Benton via private detective, via Bentons of Weston. The letter summoned him to the reading of a will.

Your presence is requested at the Offices of Carleton J. Ziskand, One Beacon St., Boston, Ma, 01201. Please attend the reading of your father's will whom passed on the 18th day of August in the year or our Lord 1997.

Benton clean, working on a dysfunctional marriage to a gal from the Tuesday night Saint Catherine's meeting, and a pair of bastard children, departed the Sunshine State to never return to its smog. And his jaw ached.

Only upon arriving in Weston did Benton learn of Mother's failing health and subsequent passing earlier in spring. Then he was told of Father's stroke, bedpans and the like. And, Father could not speak, in his last months. And Benton smiled.

"We couldn't find you when your mother died, reported the cousin now in charge of the estate. I hired a detective to serve you so you could be here for the reading of your father's last will and testament."

And so it went. "To Jonas James Benton," Gerald's only seed, a smidgeon of the entirety. And so it goes. Hate raged within the heir sitting in the office at One Beacon. Yet, he found no reason to appeal, probate, or whimper. He took the presigned check from the smiling attorney and inwardly swore off the ghosts and family of Weston. In the shining lobby of the magnificent building, he spotted the testator cousin. He waited for the alcoholic kin outside then approached him.

"If you ever contact me again I will kill you," monotone, steady, simple.

And Benton never set foot in Weston again. He would not even drive through it. And so it goes. And so it went.

Benton's dysfunctional clan lived in a house on the Belmont side of the Belmont/Cambridge line, with "the fuckin' dog," Tike. Resentments growing inside dry addict Jonas. Time to time, during the quiet of meditation, a voice would evoke, "You shouldn't get involved with the girls in the meeting," warned his sponsor. Yet Benton had made another bad decision and married her anyway.

A frigid evening '99, the bastards watching a purple dinosaur dancing on cable, Cheryl painting old kitchen cabinets, and Benton resentfully spoke at his ever expanding wife.

"I'm going out."

"Out? Where the fuck you goin' now? Why don't you spend some time with the kids?" she said in dysfunctional verbiage.

Wife ignorant of the husband's many resentments, she could not see or hear them in her own world of self-absorption. She did not know he replaced drug addiction with watching and masturbating to gay porn. Beaten, prone to beating himself, Benton looked at the bastards across the room. They did not flinch or divert their eyes from the moronic dinosaur, having heard it all before. He gave reply to his wife with the slight slamming of the door. Just enough to stir the tension.

The '93 Sable crazily drove along the snakelike curves of Storrow Drive to seek relief from Cheryl. The bastards. The fuckin' dog. Himself. AC/DC shouted Dirty Deeds Done Dirt Cheap out the cracked window. Snow fell at a lulling pace. He followed a sand truck to better grip the icy road and silently prayed to his Higher Power. Please God help me with these resentments. I know they are killing me. Please protect me in this time of discomfort. However, ice and nature gave no mind as the Sable slid down the slope into the B.U. tunnel. Now prayer ceased. Benton braced for the unknown, unseen, and unwanted. Then want appeared. Slamming the breaks made matter worse and the Sable whipped toward the yellow wall. It came to rest just prior to slamming the bricks when its wheels gripped the de-iced pavement of the tunnel's roadway. Florescent lights shone and flickered the isolated car now sitting the opposite direction. Both the Sable and Benton stared up the slope for another car or truck to speed over the ridge. Another change in mood, Benton shut his eyes as he craved a collision. Death. He shut the Sable's eyes too. They waited. When nothing came to end his doom, they circled around and headed in the proper direction.

"Fuck," he screamed at God, his deity, his heaven, then made another bad decision.

White streets pure like talcum, the Sable exited at Arlington Street, proceeded around the Public Gardens, by the Commons, the State House Dome, through the maze of streets to arrive downtown. He parked the car then entered the Purple Shamrock. And just like that, sobriety gone. All the work. All the meetings. All the commitment. All the prayer. Gone. So it goes.

After last call, he exited the establishment. He retrieved his wedding ring from his pocket and put it back on as he walked through the muck of gray city snow. Slurring and wrecked, sobriety discarded, he turned and stared at the purple sign shutting off for the night.

"Die dinosaur, die!" he screamed at the sign.

Nearing the car he pissed on a windowed building and thought, Maybe I should call Cheryl?

"Fuck that," echoed down the street of glass.

He entered the Sable and started her. Led Zeppelin roared through the alley of money and beyond. Jimmy Page still riffing as Benton turned between the Commons and Public Gardens. The muddied car veered to the far left.

"Fuck, fuck, fuck, fuck, he angrily repeated as the parking spots were marked, No Parking after 11 P.M. PERMIT PARKING ONLY

A flashback to childhood. Him and Father at the Bruins game. The game over. Walking to the car. The similar sign. The empty space. A taxi ride to a Boston City lot. Father's anger. And, "Terry O'Reilly gave Keith Magnuson a whoopin'."

Benton turned left onto Arlington and noticed three available spots.

"And, Eeny, meeny, miny, moe," he said giggling.

Deciding on miny, he backed the Sable into the space on the third attempt and did not leave a note on the scratched and dented cars. He sat there inebriated deciding what to do. He thought of the ever-expanding wife back home. The cunt, who admitted adultery with a woman she met at the nuthouse waiting room. He thought of gay porn. Of men he worked with. Of the FedEx guy. And another bad decision.

Benton entered the public park. Although clouded by grains and adrenaline, the sense of danger titillated instead of causing fear. He walked to a tree and pissed on its three hundred years of stillness, then walked deeper into the darkness on the coldest of nights. A whistle came from beyond a thicket of hedges so he walked toward it. Arriving at the other side, he smiled when noticing a man masturbating. The jacking pervert was well dressed and younger than himself. Benton walked toward him for surely it was not a cop.

79

"Hey," he said now feet from the man.

"You a cop?" the man asked continuing to play with himself.

"Nope."

"You want some of this in your ass?"

"You got a condom?" slurring Benton inquired.

"Yes," the man replied and reached into his coat.

Benton pivoted around, giggled and dropped his pants in excitement.

"I think I might have to piss first," he said looking back over his shoulder.

"What faggot?" is the last Benton heard.

The man swung viciously with a Red Sox souveigner bat. One swing proved enough as Benton fell in the snow and convulsed into seizure. The man put his own softness away and zipped up, bent down and took the wallet from the convulsing pants. He walked briskly into darkness like the arctic air.

Benton's body and mind continued to seize for a short while then like his prick went limp. He slept face down in the snow. A while later the cold awakened him. A searing pain clamped his head. Disoriented. He stood and fell back to the earth lethargic. He could not remember the man or what had happened. Then he napped.

Benton finally rose and felt the blood that soaked the back of his head, neck, shoulder, and side. Fingers caressed the welting bruise. He thought of Abraham Lincoln and lay back down to rest. As pain continued its rule, he looked around not at a park but a forest. Now Jerry Benton loomed above him in the quiet thicket of trees. Fearing another blow, he decided to rise and run. He staggered through the Public Garden and crossed into the Boston Common. Head trauma and alcohol had its way as Benton sat on a bench and shat himself. He sat there helpless and lonely feeling the submissiveness of one shitting their pants.

"What is happening?" he screamed toward the sky.

He searched for the wallet now gone. He vaguely recalled a wife, a car, the kids, a fuckin' dog.

"Fuck them too," he screamed not knowing who they were.

A homeless man peeked out from a bag and box behind the bushes.

"There's a hospital over that way. You should go there," said the nomad.

Benton staggered across the remaining Common and crossed Tremont to an idling taxi. The man lowered his window.

"Can you bring me to the hospital?" Benton pleaded.

Smelling the shit permeating the air, the man drove away as his

Christianity napped.

"Where's the fuckin' hospital?" Benton now screamed to the near empty streets.

He noticed a man walking near the Boylston T Station. Thinking it was Father, he ran the opposite way. Fear and confusion dissipated during his zigzagging trot. Anger and rage heightened. He snarled and spit blood into the gray slushy snow.

"Where's the fuckin' hospital?" he screamed again.

The arctic wind answered with its howling cold. Benton noticed a man near the Y.M.C.A.

17

Arrest

Freddie Nolan heard commotion all of which is common to the Zone, the place he called home. Titillated, a nudge prompted him to spy out the window. He quietly opened the old wooden frame and scanned up and down the street. He saw a pair of feet sticking out from behind a dumpster in the alley. Another figure ran across the street. Excited, he turned to dial 911.

Knowing Millie the Whore liked this type of fiasco, Freddie trotted down the hall for her door when a pain smacked his chest. Breathe now half, he fell to the wall and gasped. He recited the Serenity Prayer and lay down. He watched roaches and rats patter by as he drifted off to death, as he drifted off to avenge his childhood.

A short time later, a squad car speaker sporadically spoke in squawk simulation.

A husky female voice, "Car one-thirteen, Car one-thirteen! Code three. There's a possible two-seventeen in progress in and around Lowell Court. Do you copy?"

Officer Dolan tossed the scratch ticket onto the passenger seat, threw the cruiser in reverse, and headed back down LaGrange. He braked and sledded on the slushy pavement stopping just prior to the Glass Slipper. He shone the spotlight up the dark street of Tamworth. Snowflakes made the scene appear like a black and white television on a wrong channel summoning a far off station. A person jutted out of an alcove on the screen. The spotlight aimed, a suspect ran out and bolted toward Boylston. Dolan sled the car up the street to apprehend the obvious criminal. The man darted across Boylston into the alley of Head Place. Dolan skid and stopped the car in front of the Y.M.C.A., exited and gave chase.

The husky voice continued to rant, "One-thirteen where are you? Do you copy?"

Dolan entered Head Place running quick into its darkness. He tackled the culprit at the far end of the alley where the man stood caged by a gate. Administering the cuffs, the old injury throbbing, he spat on the criminal's face. When they exited the alley, a group of deviants had amassed in the street. Pimps, johns, junkies, transvestites, city workers, politicians, nomads, watched another night play out, giving most the sordid entertainment they came to see and expect.

18

Leonard Turkleton

Leonard Turkleton jumped a bus and ventured over the Tobin to catch his weekly fix of porn. He did not know it would be a night of violence for some.

Toward end of evening and money, he watched a young man collapse at a utility pole. The streets neared empty, yet, plenty action could be found. Feeling flu-like, or at minimal a cold, he walked toward public transportation to connect with the last bus to Revere. He stopped on the walk in front of one of the many peep show establishments. He looked around, at the empty street, the beckoning flickering lights, the whore way down there, the Chinese restaurant, a streetlight dead like his soul, crushed paper boxes strewn in the gutter, the gray snow, the black ice, and he looked inside himself, and decided himself a nomad.

Leonard arrived at the corner near the station. Not quite drunk, far from sober, his nipples felt as if stapled to his chest as arctic air whipped down from the Wang Center and entered his worsening bronchitis.

"This is the zone. The Combat Zone. The hotel for homeless, the daycare for addicts," spoke his artistic imagination aloud to the street.

Deciding himself hungry, Leonard crossed the street toward the all-night pharmacy. He entered its electric folding doors and walked the aisle with its shelves of dusty old cereal boxes, canned pasta and the like. Retrieving his wallet, he found four dollar-bills and another fifty-five cents in his pockets. He spotted a plastic jar of peanut butter with a bear on its label. Just enough money, but fuck what about the bus, he thought. A nomad walked by him mumbling to himself, conversing with childhood friends or the like. Leonard turned from the homeless man and quietly cried. A repressed memory surfaced. Childhood. Blocks of butter and cheese. Institutional sized cans of peanut butter. Welfare. Wanting more, getting less, in the single parented family. Scumbag Father at the racetrack. What did he look like? Why had he left? Ma instructing, Be grateful, to her Baby. But this was today and Leonard felt contempt for peanut butter. He ambled out of the store, the bear donning jar stuffed in his parka, four fifty-five still on his person.

Stragglers, hanger-ons (the truest of addicts), shuffled across the streets and alleys, pieces in a slow chess game waiting to mate. Leonard approximated his allotted time to catch the bus. With his ticket stub purchased earlier in the night, he reentered the old theater where rats lived, and men drank cheap scotch as they watched all-night porn. Bright lights winked at Leonard so he winked back. Inside the lobby, an old man bore eyes at him. The old man hoped the younger would love, or at least sex him. Leonard chuckled when thinking, Is that a jar of peanut butter in your pocket or are you happy to see me? The chuckling ceased as he wondered how much money he could make giving old men blowjobs while rats nibbled at his feet.

He entered the cinema where synthesized music played loudly as giants fucked on screen. A Hispanic man gave head to a black as the man slept in the midst of aisle one. Closer to the screen, sex addicts, and simply the lonely, crawled and pawed a younger version of themselves like maggots on the dead. Leonard watched it all and finger ate peanut butter. And like a switch, his mood changed. A flooding despair overtook him as he thought of life's totality of aloneness. He put the cap on the jar and put it in his sweatshirt pocket. He exited the cinema, its characters and claws.

The Zone now colder, he glanced up the bend of the street toward Jordan Marsh and recalled being joyous when younger. Shopping with Ma for school clothes. He pictured the happy shoppers then remembered the mumbling nomad in the all-night store. Despair escalated. He wanted out of this place. He headed up Boylston toward the more reliable Green Line at Park Street Station. Drunk, he sat a while on cold steps. Needing to piss, he turned left after the Y.M.C.A. He walked down the slope of Tamworth and noticed the blackness of an alley. An overextended bladder made stapled nipples obsolete. He entered the alley of Lowell Court and stood near the wall. An unnoticed rat watched from its perch on the rim of a dumpster, teeth stained with slime, as the Two Legger braced the wall. Leonard reached to unzip and giggled as he thought of procuring, inventing, and investing in drive-thru prostitution.

"Hey," a voice said at the mouth of the alley. "Big man."

The voice walked toward him. Startled, Leonard stepped deeper into the alley.

"You want head for twenty?" the figure asked.

Leonard's thoughts raced. Fear dissipated. Tranquility emerged as each breath begged for sobriety.

"Nah. I'm headed home, thanks."

"You sure?"

"Yeah, but thanks," Turkleton reiterated.

The dark figure reached in his pocket and produced a Swiss Army Knife, opened it, and pointed the largest blade at Turkleton's gut. Sixth grade karate class passed Leonard's mind. Was it gedan barai or age uke, the downward block? The alley he imagined a movie set.

"Then give me your fuckin' wallet," the man demanded.

"I only have a few bucks, just enough to get home."

A noise came from the dumpster and the man turned to look. Leonard grabbed for the man's arm but obesity slowed him. The man panicked, turned and jammed the knife into Leonard's gut. He then ran from the alley as the victim fell to the ground.

Leonard sat propped against the door to nowhere as urine warmed his legs and ass. He toppled and lay on the ground. Numbness overcame him as he stared toward the mouth of the alley. A pair of red eyes stared back. Leonard could not discern if he were alive or dead. I should be out buying Christmas gifts, he thought. When will God, Satan, or some angel come and get me. He lay there, throat and gut on fire. Breathing slowed as he coughed one last time. He recalled cop and fire shows instructing to leave the knife in to slow the bleeding. Before shutting his eyes to the alley and darkness, he witnessed a rat run off and the vague smell of nuts.

Leonard woke in a hospital bed wearing a speckled gown that wedged his ass. His clothes rolled up in a blue bag and a nurse stated his wallet was safe with security. He had tracheal bronchitis, a repairable stab wound, and another shot at life.

His brother walked in, "There you are," the sibling said.

Leonard smiled briefly, said hello and fell back to sleep. When he awoke, his brother was watching the muted Bruins game. Am I the only person who gets into shit like this? Leonard thought. His sister arrived with flowers and cried.

"You little bastard," she sputtered through snot, tears and spit.

The brother held her as she cried. The brother then dramatically informed Leonard how he survived the attacker.

Later, visitors gone, lights dimmed, nurses whispering at their station, Leonard Turkleton painfully rose and walked to the flowers on the windowsill. He stared at the dank street below. He cried. No longer did he have contempt for peanut butter. He later remembered that night as if it were somebody else.

19

The Burrow

Mr. and Mrs. Rat lay in their cement burrow claw in claw. The clan lay near their feet and beyond. The group spoke in turn telling their many adventures, some of which embellished. Full circle, then it was Rat's turn. All quieted and only the shaking of the bridge could be heard, as Rat never told a lie.

He told his journey of the night. How he went to the alley to eat. The Two Legger that lay smelling of nuts. The other Two Legger running off bleeding from the back of his head.

Mr. and Mrs. Rat ogled each other with gratitude.

Rat turned to the crowd and again spoke in rat gibber, "Don't worry my kin, the Two Leggers kill themselves."

Epilogue

Having seen through the eyes of rats, Leonard Turkleton never became, a Nomad of the Alley.

two short stories

The Sad Life of John Adams

The Trees

The Sad Life of John Adams

John Adams, no relation to any historical figure, lethargically strolled into the museum, an empty soul of an addict, the gait of an all night drunk. Veins and bodysuit full of resin, causing the left foot to falter the ambitions of the right, he trudged the white marble floor not knowing the reason for being there, or, if there were any at all. Euphoria had faded an hour ago and John entered the world known to most as reality. Adams handed the security guard a twenty-dollar bill. The man stood silent and stunned having never been tipped before. This is how the inherently rich "bastard" spent most days while in wait for a check from the Orient or Europe, Boston, Texas, Belize, or wherever adulterous Father lived for the while.

Lazily turning left, stumbling, he journeyed for the men's room. Once inside the pseudo-sanitized place, he proceeded to make the stall a privatized heroin hut. Too unsteady to cook, he snorted the white powder atop a fisted hand. Broken capillaries on a pimpled nose marquee to a once handsome face, sick dispersed from the teen's core. Self-pity exuded rampant like the erupting acne. Again steady, a needle and the like followed. Nodding following that. Lethargy hid for the while, life taking a nap.

The buzz now adequate, he rose revived from the opiate abyss. Attempting to walk half-reasonable, remarkably considering two bags gone, lethargic boney feet led awkwardly to the exhibition gallery. A lone cedar bench held firm when Adams quickly pivoted and crashed his anorexic ass down. So not to be taken as a junkie, he sat studious, proper, and erect. The stomach devoid of food clutched at bile inside itself. Chemicals tumbled with stolen cookies. Vague amounts of vomit, proving just enough to add to the high, had to be swallowed so not to be wasted.

"If only it could last. If only it could last," he whispered.

More life gone, Adams clutched at the bench as breathing slowed. Once secured, he scanned the room with green pinned eyes. Left, right, then back again. Over and over this was repeated. Alone he thought until spotting the camera gliding quietly above. No longer was Adams alone in the quiet art chamber.

Staring, he imagined miniscule cobwebs home to miniscule spiders, draping the back of the ocular spy. Just like Grandma making her green and white sweater, he thought. Left, right, left, right, screamed through the numbness of the numbed mind. Green eyes danced in tandem with the inebriated brain. The left eye faltered the ambitions of the right. The green pair then nodded to the pestering voice. Finally the doped mind fell to a junkie heaven.

Gazing upward, no longer did he notice a camera but a Cyclops. Distorted thoughts chatted to each other to rationalize a guard living within the monster. The junkie's demeanor changed. He gawked forward as if awed by the, until then unseen, breathtaking art. The following moments changed the addict's life.

On the vast egg-white wall hung a painting entitled Spring. It was part of a traveling exhibit from the famed Getty Museum. Adams stood and walked slowly toward the masterpiece. His wetted eyes now finally aligned, he stood transfixed at the black petitioning bar. The camera continued to search for belligerence and theft.

From the rear of Cyclops, a thin black wire traveled to a bored hole in the egg-white wall. The troglodyte wire slithered through aluminum corridors until exiting another wall. Several feet below sat, to anyone who would listen, a self-proclaimed "Hero." The gregarious guard binged on pizza and M.S.G. chips. He sat with his back to the monitor where the wire ended its slack. His drug of choice chased with "Goooood Voodka" and a belching respite. He did this to forget Korea. With oversized fluid-encased fingers, he brushed specks of fatty drippings and flakes from the polyester blue. The gregarious guard's lack of work ethic, Cyclops gliding along, John Adams was left alone.

The 911 bus inched its way over the Tobin Bridge hacking smoke signals to Boston and her surroundings. A pair of camouflaged legs jumped from the steps of the choking transport at Haymarket Station. Half laced scuffed Army boots ran down into the subway. The Green Line train would bring Adams to a 5 o'clock appointment with a man he considered a Nazi. He was clean for the moment knowing Doctor Grasso would not take any shit. "Whatsoever."

Upon entering the shrink's psychoparlour, his stomach gripped. Adams feared the supposed Nazi he nicknamed "Goood Doctor" in exaggerated German dialect. However, at the time the teen did not know that the short stern man sitting across from him served in the same war as the security

90

guard. Nor would he care. Understandably, Adams did not know how on one chaotic night, latter '50s, the future therapist would enter a dark, cold forest. Suddenly black-black trees restored to flickering mint green as rockets and gunfire sprayed the battalion. Eighteen-year-old Grasso stood to watch the Fourth of July sky. How wonderful the colors and this thing called hashish, the soldier thought. Adams could not know the trio of problems generated that night. Firstly, it was not the Fourth of July. Secondly, the slivers of shrapnel that ripped the left baby maker from the right. Concluding, everything unbalanced, the creation of the Good Doctor's anger.

When Daddy Adams searched to remedy his little bastard son, Doctor Grasso came highly recommended by another fellow-pioneering Harvard freak. Rules were set at the initial family consult when the Adams family met the bitter dwarf-like man.

"If John misses more than two sessions his allowance will be cut," balding father said to the nut.

Young Adams adhered. Weekly he listened to Grasso lecture on pubescent punks and their attitudes, responsibilities and expectations to the masses. One session, spit emanating at odd intervals, the Good Doctor explained away his Fourth of July in Korea to end with a forty-five minute monologue on patriotism, Vietnam and the like. During the testicular testimony, Adams decided he would never trust the nutless gnome who seemingly towered slightly higher than his own crotch.

"Sooo, how are we today Johnny ?" rhetorically posed the Hummel sitting between the oak desk and plagued wall bragging Ivy League, courage and service.

"Okay," replied the passive youth in Harvard Square drawl.

"Your father called me today wanting to know if you're alright."

Pause.

"Jesus H. when will you visit him? You need him if you know what I mean?"

Anger pierced, nearing scream, "Well?" the spouting midget demanded of the pimpled teen.

Adams said nothing, left foot tapping slower than a clock, slower than the lightest of snow passing by the same psyche window in winter. Adams then departs. Session concluded, Grasso shifts in his leather seat trying to balance his bag, feeling the pain of phantom limb.

The next day rose slowly from the warming ocean into another humid sweat. Boston lay sluggish in the pestering sun. Some believed she was burning herself into the Book of Revelations.

From Christian talk radio a hyper-vigilant evangelist proclaimed, "If Sodom and Gomorrah exists, it is here."

Asthmatics scurried for inhalers while drag queens tunneled virus to unprotected johns. The gods lethargically shuttered for another summer day in Beantown.

John Adams had one best friend, an only friend at that. Nicknamed in reference to his physical size, mouse-like, his name was Mousey. In this friend's room, Adams lay in sweat on and in a vinyl, prehistoric beanbag. Mister and Misses Mouse had departed the Tudor home for their incorporated American nuclei. Before leaving, Misses Mouse placed her son's allowance in the familiar antique library table. Vivacious Mouse was ignorant that this would become dope money for her doted upon "Little Baby." The friends slept unmoving sustained by a nocturnal fix of top shelf drugs available to the well to do and impoverished alike. Akin to the children's fable, Mommy Mouse was indeed blind.

Adams woke first while unheard blue jays squawked. He trudged ding-toed through the shag rug toward the apneic mouse. Lurking above his only friend, green eyes filled preparing a guttural sob. He dropped his stubbly chin to the boney chest and wailed.

Mousey entered the wasting day fogged and concerned.

"What's up?" asked the mouse.

The much taller teen placed his wet face into nail bitten hands. The mouse's concern increased with each heightening sob.

"What up J, you alright? You still trippin' or somethin'?"

Eyes locked. Crying dissipated.

Demanding, an order, "I want you to just stay there Mousey. I want to you to lay there and listen to me like you've never done before."

The supine friend did as ordered while trying to ignore the flu-like symptoms thought to be dope sickness.

Uninterrupted, Adams confessed, "I've known you a while Mouse. And, like some fuckin' song, I feel I've known you forever. Without doubt you are my best friend."

Fearing the rise and potentially debilitating nag of hesitation, Adams closed his eyes and continued, "The other day I was at the museum and saw the Getty Exhibit. Yes, I was high on that stuff you gave me for my birthday. But it was in that place, a mere moment of time, my life changed. Like a poem or something. I felt the opposite end of a heart being crushed or mangled. The opposite of alone or depressed. All when I laid eyes on the painting Spring."

Adams then paused feeling flu-like himself. Mousey stared at the raving confessor while enduring his devotion to quiet and still. John Adams then turned and walked across the cluttered clothed marshland. He pressed a power button and upped the volume to an eventual promise of deafness. Mousey lay there fetal, achy, wondering if he knew the emoting confessor at all. Adams then turned down the bass pounding Bach.

"Did you hear that my friend? Did you hear the beauty of the bouree? You know as well as I, that at one time I could find beauty in Bach. Now he is dead!" Adams sadly exclaimed.

Then excited, "At the museum I saw a painting, or it saw me, that moved me more than one did Dorian Gray. Remember that one from school Mouse? The one by Oscar Wilde? The guy and the painting? I was moved Mouse. Now I will tell you why."

Adams sucked in the stale drug den air and splurged ahead, "In that picture there was a dude about our age, maybe a year or younger. He was playing a flute. Handsome in a way I've never known a man to be."

Sweating Adams confessed, "Mousey, I cried because he reminded me of another."

Pause.

Birds chirped away. Autos sped down Route 9. Hamburger defrosted on the kitchen counter.

"It was you."

Adams stood firm no longer shifting weight between left and right foot. Staring at his friend, the friend did nothing. Eyes locked. Mousey suspected, almost convinced, something bad was about to occur. Unsure of his safety, he grimaced and squinted his dark brows to eclipse his own pinned eyes. Nostrils widened stretching the acne on his own pimpled nose. Then he smiled. The mouse rose and walked to his friend.

Grabbing Adams at the shoulders, he jubilantly exclaimed, "Man, that was good shit I did when you were sleeping! Want some?"

John Adams froze astonished. His eyes remained wet like fresh oils on a painter's brush. Jaw muscles clenched, green-eyed slits of fury. Having just come out of the closet, having professed his love, rejected in the same moments, his face began to resemble that of a murderer. Burning red eyes gazed at a far off horizon of nothingness. Now, for all Adams cared, Mousey could shoot himself into a coma.

Hamburger continued to melt.

A belching taxi escorted John Adams back to the museum. First things first, twelve-steppingly thought, as he headed for his privatized crack house. His bobblehead was escorted atop a now stable gait. He stuck the needle in the jugular to reach the quickest attainable height.

Again Adams crashed onto the cedar bench. Refusing to be cognitive, he walked over to Spring. Lethargic left foot followed the right like the Cyclops above. Tremulous, he reached into his wrinkled vest pocket. Fear rose inside his belly, throat, and mind. It rose from the primal inside him. The abyss. The dope. The stomach began to clench and Adams froze. He stared at Spring and it stared back. Suddenly he understood Dr. Grasso's Fourth of July night. Of the fear that can arise, the anger that quietly ruminates way down. John Adams giggled while remembering the Good Doctor's anger regarding the tainted testicle. Then instantly his eyes bore a malevolent gaze at the flute player. The rest of the masterpiece became a backdrop of sorts.

Cyclops quietly hummed, left right, left right. The quivering hand steadied as he jerked it out of the vest pocket. The syringe, the shared needle, a vector of virus, now clutched in his sweated hand glistening under man made illuminations of light. Now delusion made him notice a shimmer of sun reflecting off the drop of liquid at the needle's point. He fantasized of Mousey's ejaculation. Adams did not know the virus traveled in each.

A congregation of chemicals swam and swirled within the liquid making Adams bigger than life, so he thought. He reminisced of the euphoria it had once brought. Like a veil, sadness covered his face for he knew it was something else he craved. John Adams wanted to experience unconditional love, the love he lost when Mother died. He then remembered losing his virginity in a Combat Zone parking lot to a whore named Gina. Or was it Tina? he quickly debated.

Primary to all was his insatiable yearning to be loved by Mousey or Daddy Adams. He dreamed of holding hands with Mousey at the Kendall

94

Cinema. He dreamed of living in a quiet house with Father where flowers grew, Italian Greyhounds running free. These he craved more than dope, so he thought.

Confused, Adams stared at the character within the painting that brought him to these deductions the day before. The Flute Player marched triumphantly and confident in front of others upon the oiled sketch.

"Probably the celebration of Spring," Adams whispered to his isolation.

The subject's shiny black hair reminded him of Mousey. They look remarkably alike, he thought. He remembered the passing conversation with the doorman the prior day.

"My man, how does one go about purchasing one of the delightful pieces inside?" he asked the tired student employee, almost Master in Engineering to fill the baby's bottle.

"Forgetit mahn, the Gettys and the Foundation are not hard pressed for moooney these daaayz," he said donning filmed tired eyes. "They are never sold!"

In the midst of heroin high, John Adams knew it to be a lost cause. He would never own or love the Flute Player he adored.

Adams, who encompassed an unquenched thirst for love of the same gender, stared blankly at the masterpiece now inches away. Suddenly he was prompted to the here and now of the museum. Pounding of feet way over there. Left right! Left right! He imagined it to be the Good Doctor or the Nazi Party coming to escort him to Dostoyevsky's Russia. He slowly lifted his black dilated eyes and stared at the Flute Player with resentment, with disgust, with longing. The Cyclops stood steady, staring down upon the homicidal man. It stared down on malevolence; a lonely person with an unmet desire. No one would ever have the delusion he loved.

The left rights became louder and pounded in time with his heart. Quickly, compulsively jealous, Adams raised the syringe high above himself. A small pond flew from the needle's tip in a glistening arc that plummeted to the marble floor. It shattered into smaller and smaller hits for spiders to snort later. He took aim and closed his black eyes. The left rights continued to echo louder and louder. Adams peered through slitted eyes for the final time at his love. The rest of the masterpiece gone, part of the non-existing room. Now the Flute Player, the vibrating echo, and hatred remained.

Off in the distance someone yelling, pleading for the life of the intended victim. The right triceps quivered and tightened. The weapon brought downward into the neck of his lover, harsh, wild, ripping at the entire art world. A cackle, then John Adams whispered into the ear of the Flute Player, "I loved you."

While Adams hysterically laughed, a portly guard tackled the teen and pinned him with a Korean Conflicted knee. The junkie smiled and spat on the marble floor's starry starry shine.

Several months later, John Paul, no relation to any Getty or Pope, Adams performed the last leg of community service. Per order of the Commonwealth, Dear Daddy Adams was forced to purchase the desecrated Spring. The security guard and doorman of the museum often had coffee together after long, long shifts driving taxi. Doctor Grasso duly terminated for incompetence.

Two years from the day of the stabbing, Mister and Misses Mouse sat in the office of the maddened midget. Mister Mouse often held the blotched hand of his now matronly wife. She told the midget of the withering of their only child. Of the sores on his now anorexic-like back. Of the rotating nurses who were being paid to empty the forever filling bedpan.

Shortly after, Adams attended the funeral of his only friend who eventually died of an overdose of pain meds, not the virus that riddled his soul. Yet, either way, John Adams thought it was he who caused the death of the mouse. Withering himself, John Adams drove home and went directly to his room.

Sitting on the edge of the bed, he laid out paraphernalia beside his boney thigh. As tears and joy again filled his green eyes, he admiringly stared at Kurt Cobain on the wall. As ponds, upon ponds of chemicals emptied into the blue and red rivers, John Adams drifted more and more beyond the distance, while Bach played at a fevering pitch.

The Trees

Where hills slowly inclined to become mountains, and these masses of earth went forever higher and leaned as if to kiss, I searched for truth. I needed to do this for love ceased to be attainable, and life had become mundane after a traumatic summer of a most harsh and harrowing time. I was twenty-eight years old.

My journey brought me to the enticing act of contemplating nature. After a long day of hiking, getting higher and higher like the earth itself, I ended upon a ridge. Never shall I disclose its locale for it is a holy ground of sorts to me. At the time I considered the journey spiritual. I know better now. Atop the ridge of this particular mountain I transcended the reality that I had previously inhabited.

The view was splendid indeed. Glancing at the tundra of the far off lands and the opaque reddening skies, I began to ponder all types of things. I thought of god, man, and the great hereafter. What Carlton Fisk did the night before in the World Series meant nothing, nor, where my soon to be ex-wife would be living or how she would survive the cruel and empty world. My mind concentrated on the deeper level of surrealism. At the same time I knew my mind to be on a ridge of its own, fault like; soon to slide into a hell that barely compared to one specific morning of the previous summer. As the brisk autumn air shaved my face, a decision was made. At that precise moment I named the ridge Tree Truth Pass. It is where I had thought to have found truth or at least a semblance of peace. I was wrong.

Before I get deeper into the telling of my journey, let me begin the telling of that summer day, the morning that was the opening to my nadir.

It was early morning when I awoke next to my wife in the cottage we rented annually for our vacation. I grabbed some milk and medicinals. Sounding like hoofs of a Clydesdale, my feet clopped down the hill headed for the lake. Crickets sawed behind me in four four time. As it always was, and most likely remains to be, Newfound Lake was pristine. There was the familiar slapping of water at the sides of the floating dock anchored thirty yards out. Barely skirting the tree lines on top of the most eastern mountain, the sun hinted another appearance promising purple rays upon this peaceful place.

I sat tentative onto the familiar red and white lounge chair that held steady for the moment. With addictive fervor I ingested the milk and medicinal. Once again they became peripatetic finding their way through my stomach to reach my overworked mind. I thanked god I was not drinking for a handful of no longer consuming alcoholics had recently convinced me of being one of their kind. Soon enough drool made my chest hair shine.

I glanced around and found life to be beautiful, simply beautiful. Through slick lips I whistled the 1800 Overture while reminiscing the many Fourths with Arthur Fiedler. With my left hand thrashing about, I mimed the dead conductor. The red and white squeaked below my fattening ass as if to say, Let me be. I am soon to retire with the State, let me be. I reached for more of my drugs.

I stopped my thrashing and began drifting to sleep. Not long thereafter I heard the sound of an angel, a true angel. From half way up the hill, or down, chose your liking, I heard the slapping of his sneakers on the old paved hill. My only child. My joy. My truest love. God.

My toes began to numb beneath the cold gold miniscules of sand. I peered across the lake to notice a small cottage sitting secluded between multitudes of trees. Often I had thought of swimming to the other side but imagined it to be excessively far. The wind was blowing the lake to the right, or left, mattering which beach you stood upon. The small waves of the lake made little noise yet seemed to be hissing. Hissing as if to taunt. Hissing again. The dock slapping back at the dark blue, black water.

Standing there with a fantastic smile of glee, hazel eyes of his mother, God kicked off his sneakers.

"And what gets you up so early?" I inquired of God.

"Want to go for a swim Dad?"

It would turn out, as my wife slept soundly in the old bed, god slept too.

I must stop writing at this time. Once again, I am being called up to the house.

As I stared down from the edge of my newly discovered Pass, my bloodshot eyes engulfed a river below that resembled the veins of my wrist, frigid-blue. Forty feet across the ravine sat another ridge that mirrored the Pass. Whereas Tree Truth Pass contained boulders of different sizes, the color of the graying sky, the other side was aesthetically more pleasing with its red clay and towering oaks. It was some kind of paradise. I named that side Eternity Landing.

At the center of the Pass as if posing for a portrait, hauntingly stood a pair of trees twenty feet from each other. Gravel-like earth covered their roots. This place, I imagined, resembled the outskirts of an old western town. Ragweed and twigs were strewn about like hairs on a Barber's floor, pirouetting with the wind that chilled my depression set mind. The last of the mauve sky crushed by clouds of coal. To my misfortune, I can remember all of this as if yesterday.

At odd intervals of time, I heard what sounded like the shuffling of feet. I frowned having hoped to be alone in this magnificent place; alone with my mind.

Pivoting to the west, I was spooked by the pair of trees that were darkening with the sky and my subsequent affect. These barked ones stood isolated like myself, dust at their roots and my feet. We tried to appear strong in the midst of the oncoming storm. As I gazed at the trees in the last hour of daylight, the darkening sky made clear to me that god was closing his eyes once again.

The tree on the right was much larger than its neighbor and tenfold the size of the oaks on the Landing. Bewitchingly robust, it stood proud posing for the last remnants of daylight. Its enormous trunk was beige with black cracks running up its devilish skin. At the top, the beige dissipated to become black which shot out into strong, threatening branches. I became so mesmerized that I no longer felt the chill of the late October sketch.

Two-thirds the size of its towering neighbor, bark flat gray approximating wood after a campfire, the tree to the left was undoubtedly less palatable. Its one and only branch jutted out from its pathetic side reaching just beyond the edge of the Pass. The tiny arthritic end pointed east like a compass high above the forever-flowing, frigid-blue river. I walked lethargically to the base of the larger tree and sat against it to rest. My wiry back fit nicely against its welcoming trunk. The trees appeared to be readying for a dance, the larger one's rotunda obviously would lead.

Across the ravine, moose, deer, rabbit and hare appeared motionless, catatonic. Enormous black hawks perched on branches high above me. I felt the earth shake but rationalized this to be my exhaustion. While feeling nothing I began to think of my childhood. Then I napped for a brief time. Later I set up camp between the two trees and finally lay down for the night. I stared lucidly into space for an unaccountable period. I thought myself to be a star, shimmering, full of extreme heat. A fever overtook me, so I thought. A heightening panic filled me as I tried to sleep. This state brought on, I believe, by the awareness of my reality, the debit of my life's totality. My mind reluctantly drifted off, off, to sleep while an angry wind whipped below the freckling of stars.

A peck on my shoulder catapulted me to my feet rattling my temporary home. As I reached for the flashlight, cricket-like sounds became louder and louder then droned to what I discerned to be a whisper. Frozen in horror, tremulously my body shook along with the ray of light my hand held to cut through the onslaught of blackness. Then I noticed them for the first time, giant squirrels. Ten or more I quickly estimated. One pattered toward me on hind legs in the shivering ray of light.

Silver about three feet tall like a huge water rat, he spoke, My name is Enogib.

When I heard the King's English I became vertiginous and faded out.

He stood next to me when I came to. Afraid to move, questioning my sanity, I asked him a question,

Are you really there, or, have I gone insane?

I thought I heard laughter. He flipped backward through the circus-lit air the speed of syrup to land on his hind legs a few moments later. His burly body rolled on the dusty earth back and forth between the other squirrels and me. My eyes adjusted to the darkness to notice many more of his kind. He then squealed a very high pitch. A smile placated below his pudgy snout. His eyes bore through me. The laughter became nervous as if a comedian bombing on stage. Becoming vertiginous again, I willed myself not to fade off.

A thunderous clap lazered through my frontal bone to the occipital lobe, a deafening crackle that filled my head with pressure. Seconds later a branch crashed down from the larger tree. The squirrels trembled, so did I. Smiles disappeared like the stars.

Hide me in your pack and move to the other tree we call Taerg, the one colored gray, he said quickly.

It all felt surreal as I ventured into a new realm. Numbness replaced by chaos, it is the former I prefer to this day. I no longer questioned my sanity.

Underneath the tree named Taerg, Enogib gently sat on hind legs. His black bear-like nose crinkled on his pudgy round face with childlike curiosity. He told me a legend. It went and goes something like this.

When large birds soared and roared and nestled here on this mountain all could speak including water. The wind sang, the sun buzzed, the moon hissed like a snake. Silver squirrels were many, thousands. During these centuries, two brother trees grew atop the mountain. The squirrels named them Loof and Taerg.

During the tedious process of evolution, the mountain was split in half by the tremendous force of a river. Being constantly fed by torrential rains, the river grew stronger along with the brother trees. While most animals remained on Eternity Landing, squirrels and hawks apocalyptically remained on the Pass with the brothers.

Enogib continued.

The squirrels turned silver over time in order to survive the ever-hungering black hawks. In the sun or moonlight, their silver coats would reflect brightly and blinding. Confused of the actual position of their prey, the rapacious, devious hawks plummeted to an earthly grave. This became disdainful for the hawks soon enough and they learned to wait for the rains. Rain would darken the coats of the silver squirrels, thus, a sentence of death to most.

Loof and Taerg were created when an eagle dropped seed upon the mountain. Wind, sun, and water promised the growth of the brother trees. Beautifully jejune they were to all who witnessed them. The squirrels knew it destiny, this existence of the brothers; a sonnet to be played, a waltz to be danced.

One day it was noticed by a prestigious hawk named Bubezleeb that Loof was growing at a much quicker rate than his homely, pathetic sibling. The large black hawk proudly decided to rest on Loof's top branch, at the top level, at the feet of heaven. He convinced other hawks to join him by promising them top of the world. Bubezleeb is spawning still.

Loof grew stronger from the added weight of the black birds eventually outgrowing his brother by hundreds of feet. Remaining fact until the current day, Loof forever remained larger.

The pudgy one continued.

Each dawn as the sun crept up the backside of the mountain, warming the exiting night chill and drying the rains, Loof shined amber and crimson from uniquely painted leaves. The reflection travelled great distances because of his growing size and position on the mountaintop. Most marveled at the sight and soon thought Loof to be a god. Demonically the seasons had to change, leaves had to whither.

Taerg was soon a third of his brother, an inkling at Loof's itching side. Each passing season brought more and more sorrow to the pathetic appearing tree. The trunk turned gray and roots became brittle, forever constricted in a dance of death with his brother's stronger roots. Now a nuisance at Loof's side, a twig readied to snap, most peered at him with disgust. The squirrels were wiser."

Then I awoke, I thought, surrounded by dozens of silver squirrels four feet tall. They spoke in a rapid chatter often squeaking and squealing, professing their fears. My head twirled. Delirium must be soon. No longer could I decipher whether I was awake or sleeping, alive or dead. The ever-nagging question of sanity was not brought up again. Past and present the same, I became part of, or at least felt as if inside, the legend of Tree Truth Pass. Surrealism was no longer an oddity. It just was, and so was I. Most things seemed foreign and new but for the parallel panic both the squirrels and I experienced in our detached minds. Reality or the like slipped away and I faded out.

Gregarious wings spanned above us amidst the charcoal sky. A dim moon dangled high above, scanning down on us, a spotlight microscopically showboating death itself. Wearing no smile, frown, or any noticeable affect or salutation, the moon bellowed out a shriek. That of a tortured cat. Fear heightened inside my newfound friends and me. Taerg shook.His bark weeped. The rains were soon to come and its ugly dance partner death would be accompanying her. The animals on Eternity Landing held fast to watch fate have its way once again. Sharpening their claws and devious minds, ugly malevolent hawks screeched with anticipatory delight.

Enogib, knowing the needs of his own, tried to comfort us all by continuing with the Legend. He continued to explain why squirrels became so enchanted with Taerg.The whole while I was becoming, became, was and was not the Legend. Enogib and I told the story that was both past and present. I was both narrator and participant. Everything had enmeshed, reality, surrealism, sanity and its opposites. And as I had feared, the narrator would fade and all would become a moment in time. One long, insane sketch, painted by god's angry palette and paints. The legend continued hereditary like father to son...

Over the centuries while Loof outgrew his forever-miniaturizing brother, the former berated and heckled the latter. Hawks cackled from the top branches of the malevolent tree, egging on their hero, their mentor, their god. Demoralization and belittlement, constriction of his fragile roots by the stronger homicidal brother, Taerg submitted only to help the squirrels. Yet, Taerg always forgave his brother and the pain in the ass - vulture - wannabes. Forgiving at least in demeanor. Knowing a larger canvas to be painted, than to live out the wishing and gnawing of hate that dwelled inside, hounding at his mind sporadically as it does to us all, Taerg continued his days as if all was well.

Rains accompanied destruction. With humbleness and honor, Taerg welcomed squirrels into his hollow trunk. They were smaller than two feet then. Soon they were larger than the capacity of the safe warm place. Whoever did not make it inside the cocoon became victim to the ever-multiplying hawks.

Like insult to injury, matters became worse for the pudgy faced ones. Brittleness, brought upon by the rooted constrictions of his brother, Taerg's branches often fell to the earth maiming or killing his little silver friends. Yet, the squirrels never resented their god. They hugged him while singing his favorite Psalms. Euphoria replaced despair.

The sky heated to dark black and crimson. A thunderous clap awoke me, or put me to sleep, I could not tell. Animals settled at the edge of the Landing to grieve their friends in the hour of death. Cutting the dome-like crimson sky mingled clouds of doom. The tragedy I supposed about to happen would surely be too much for my mind, I thought. Hysterical, I ran crazily to the edge wanting to jump to the river below and my untimely death. Rain. Water. These pummeled my world once again.

I screamed as squirrels scattered to extend their precious lives. Sorrowful, I peered at Taerg and cried like I've never known. Loof convulsed with laughter while hawks readied on their perch, eager to descend from their high mighty place.

Like a team of consorted evildoers, the black winged bastards dove at their gray colored prey. My friends became confused in the midst of this horror show running into each other as claws ripped upon them. In the midst of hell, my friends scuttled toward their barked ally. The trunk filled quickly.

Others climbed upward for the lone branch that simulated a runway toward the Landing, their only hope. Like a parade of the dying, my friends ran determined to the end of the branch and leaped for their lives. A few made it to the other side while the rest fell to the deadly black river that soon turned red.

The last attempt was that of Enogib. With wounds on his furry back and neck, he gazed at me with piercing hazel eyes, as if I was his only love, his only hope, his god. I closed my eyes as his tiny feet shuffled on the wilting branch. He ran slowly headed for the oncoming waves of disaster, and beyond to a larger peaceful existence. I tried to convince myself this was true. Still I can't recall reality. This final scene evades me as if to save myself from the last leap, the last plunge into nothingness.

Hawks began to screech not having had their final serving of greed. Horrific sounds wailed through the cloud shaded moonlit air as my little friends were demolished. A repetitive numbing rain etched an affect into my mood I cannot forget even 'til this day. I stood in front of Taerg's branch with a rope and decided how I would deal with it all. No longer did I want god to determine my fate or decisions. As I tightened the noose, Enogib let out a sorrowful scream from a place I could not see. A scream that seemed distant like the waves of a lake while one lazes on the beach half-awake and half-comatose.

I awoke to daylight on the mountain, alone again, a hollowness in me that has never left. I sobbed then quickly fell asleep, the only reality I could bear.

The episode mentioned above preceded my trip to this place. I write this some two and a half decades later. The Good Doctor who is treating me during my stay came up with a new strategy to help me remember the past. One fine day he summoned me up to the house. He handed me a notebook and pen.

"Now try to remember Mister Blake. Try to remember."

Imagine. The stupid bastard far from understands my situation. I do not want to remember the past.

Directly I was sent to this celebrated institution after found roaming the mountain in a delirious state. Allowed to stay not because I am of an extreme case, but simply because of my financial health.

I choose to remain here because of the unending supply of quietness and medicines that help me to sleep. That is the only time in which I do not think

104

of that brutal summer morning, the day that far outweighs that of my total collapse upon the mountain.

Most days are spent with my gray beard pressed against, and mixing, with the vast green lawn of this famous nuthouse. Contempt and resentment are catalyst for my occasional inappropriate outbursts of anger usually set off when a patient walks by upsetting my lazing routine.

Everyone greets me when they pass my lawn. They call me Squirrel Man. Hospital Security does not like me feeding the squirrels but I do anyway. Four squirrels come to me each day. I named them North, South, East and West. Although, in all sincerity, I do not know which is which. I am still hollow inside. In writing this memory, I spelled some of the names backwards. I did this because the doctor is dyslexic. Imagine that, a Harvard man with dyslexia?

Now and then I think of Tree Truth Pass. The Good Doctor has labeled my time on the mountain as some kind of episode, "A break from reality." A break that was surely due to come about after having lost my God.

My resentments are deeper still. Before that sorrowful morning when God drowned, I had been attending Alcoholics Anonymous at the prodding of my wife. I know now that I was never an alcoholic but addicted to food. However, I let the pathetic men of those meetings convince me that I was one of them. Hence, I did everything they suggested. One of them being to eat. Eat! And so there I was in what turned out to be my darkest hour, eating like a pig and nodding off to a comatose like state induced by a half dozen or so donuts while my son went into the lake.

Now all I want to do is sleep. The drugs are working once again. As I ready to place down the pen, clouds hover above and a very light drizzle is spraying my face. A lone branch of an old tree whispers to me, and birds cackle as I long for sleep.

Now I lay me down to sleep,
I pray to God, my wandering sheep.
If I should die before I wake,
We'll take a swim at Newfound Lake.

www.ingramcontent.com/pod-product-compliance
Lightning Source LLC
Chambersburg PA
CBHW050832180626
46814CB00004B/1581